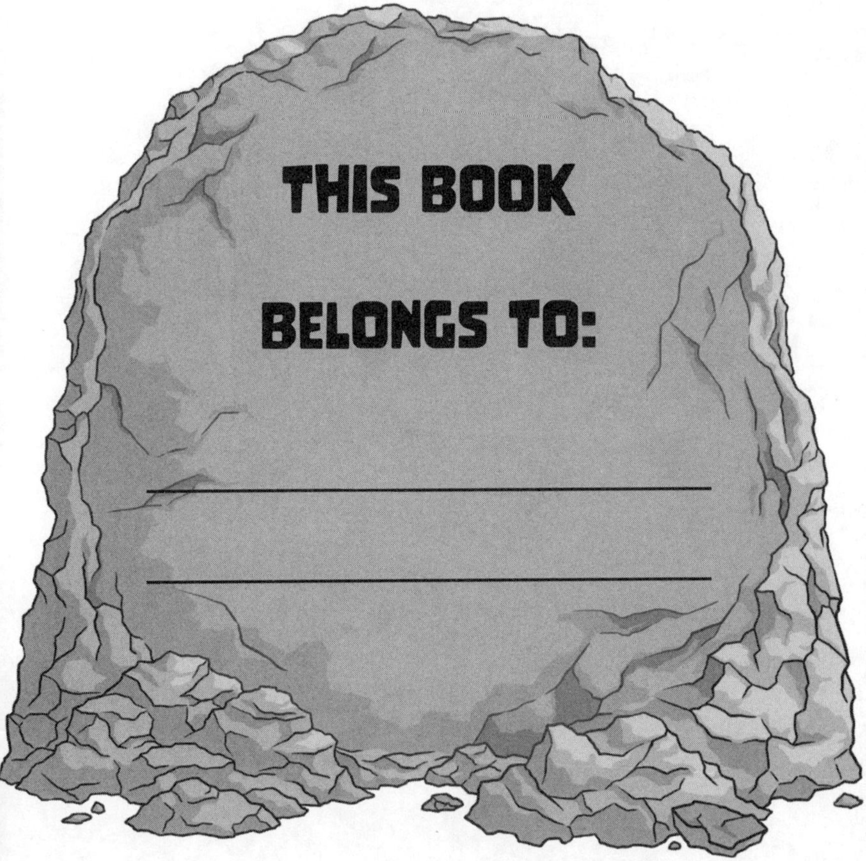
THIS BOOK
BELONGS TO:

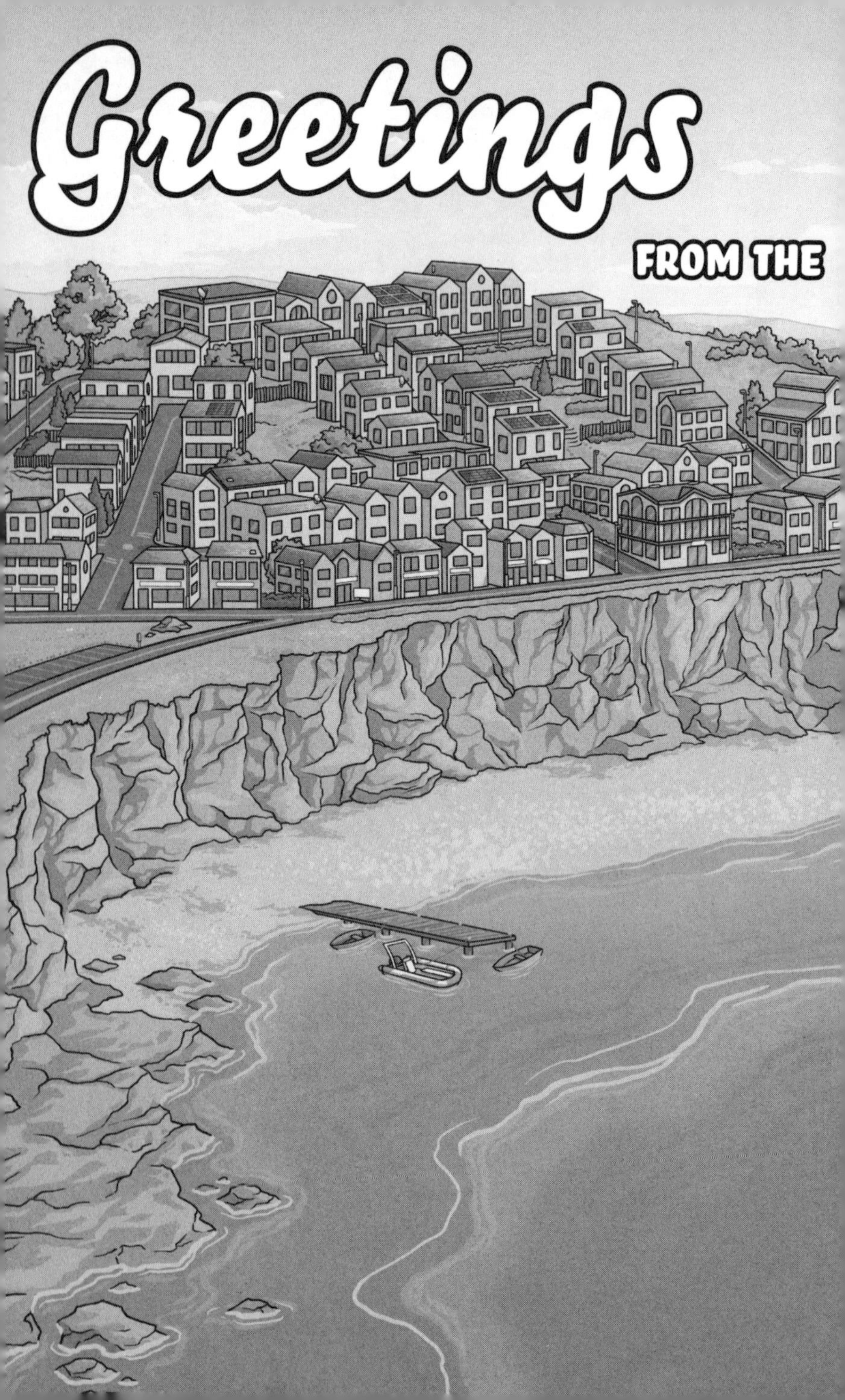
Greetings
FROM THE

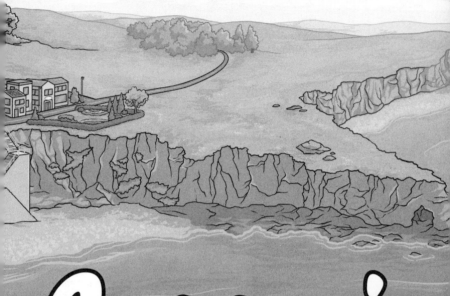

Jurassic Coast

First published 2020 © Twinkl Ltd of Wards Exchange,
197 Ecclesall Road, Sheffield S11 8HW

ISBN: 978-1-8381906-6-8

We're passionate about giving our children a sustainable future, which is why this book
is made from Forest Stewardship Council® certified paper. Learn how our Twinkl Green
policy gives the planet a helping hand at www.twinkl.com/twinkl-green.

Printed in the United Kingdom.

10 9 8 7 6 5 4 3 2 1

A catalogue record for this book is available from the British Library.

Twinkl is a registered trademark of Twinkl Ltd.

A TWINKL ORIGINAL

PHYLLIS AND THE FOSSIL FINDERS

Twinkl Educational Publishing

CONTENTS

CONTENT

Chapter One

"At least two good things about a storm: more game progress online for now, and a better chance of fossil-finding later," Jacob said with a grin as he adjusted the headset on his ears.

"Yeah, I'm with you on the first one of those, Jay. You're still on your own for the second, though!" Faizal chuckled.

"D'you think this rain is *ever* going to stop?" Nakeisha moaned as her avatar ransacked the corridors of a newly discovered stronghold and collected more glowing fire opal.

Outside Jacob's window, water ran down the seaside village road in rapid streams. Below the steep cliffs, the sea pounded the bay with ferocious waves.

"Doesn't seem like it! Feels like it's been chucking it down for weeks," said Faizal. He was following Nakeisha's character on her path of destruction through the fortress in their online game, *Raider's Peril.* They had been playing for hours that morning already.

"Actually," Jacob chipped in via his microphone, "the storm arrived on Wednesday night so it's only been two-and-a-bit days. The TV forecast said it should have passed by now. I'm pretty sure it will stop eventually." He glanced out through the window at the swirling black sky over the coast. He admired the view from his 'den', where his computer was set up.

Having no brothers or sisters meant that the spare room in Jacob's house was something that his friends all envied. Books lined the shelves along one entire side, and his dinosaur and fossil posters covered most of the opposite wall. Every available surface was crowded with dinosaur models, remains of science experiment kits or Jacob's rocks and shells. His hamsters, Steg and Rex, even had rocks and shells inside their cage. All three of his best friends liked playing *Raider's Peril;* only Jacob was such a big fan of science, though.

"OK, Mister Weatherman, we get it." Faizal's voice laughed through everyone's headphones. "Where's Gabi, anyway? Didn't she say that she'd be online again this morning?"

"Gone for another hospital check-up with her stepmum," said Nakeisha. "Said she's been feeling really tired and dizzy again this week. Reckoned she'd be done by lunch, though, so she'll probably be back any time now. I hope we can go outside again when she is."

"Feels like we're just not as effective without her on here. Hope she's OK," said Faizal as their characters raided treasure chests in an underground dungeon. "Anyone thought of a new guild name for us yet?"

Jacob had pitched his idea before but wasn't ready to let it drop yet. "I still think 'Fossil Finders Four' is the coolest," he said.

Faizal shot him down. "Not that again. Maybe if we were *all* fossil finders and not just you!"

Jacob's thumb was poised over the joystick on his controller, ready to grab a topaz spear from the stronghold wall. Before he got the chance, however, his head spun sideways towards the den window again. A jagged fork of lightning zipped through the sky and flashed through the blur of midday rain. The lightning connected with the headland along the bay and vanished into the mist again as quickly as it had arrived.

"Woah! Anyone else see that?" shouted Faizal.

"Wicked lightning!" Nakeisha responded.

Jacob had dropped his controller into his lap and squeezed his hands under his headphones to avoid hearing the deep rumble of thunder that followed. His eyes were squeezed shut and he pulled his chin into his chest.

He counted to ten, to be sure that the sound had

stopped. Tentatively, he peeled open one eye then the other. He slid his hands out from under his earphones.

Before he had a chance to pick up his controller again, the screen in front of him crackled and then turned black.

He blinked.

He tapped the side of the screen. Nothing.

There was no red light showing on the console and no voices coming from his headphones. *The power must have gone off,* he thought. Just when they were making such great progress in *Raider's Peril.*

Within moments, the doorbell rang. Jacob ran downstairs to answer it.

"Nakeisha! How d'you get here so quick?"

"What, from three doors away?" she quipped with a wide grin as she stepped inside. She gave her textured black hair a quick shake. As she was taller than Jacob, he got a brief shower from the drips that were flung from her tightly curled locks. "Power off here, too?" His friend closed the door behind herself as she breezed into Jacob's kitchen and plonked herself on a stool at the breakfast bar.

Jacob followed, taking off the headset that he was still wearing. "That game probably won't have saved properly with the power going off so suddenly, you know. The autosave will have happened before we completed that last raid," he said.

"Chill, Jacob. We'll nail it again later," Nakeisha smiled as she flicked through his *Young Palaeontologist* magazine on the countertop. Jacob watched her glance straight past an awesome article all about Ichthyosaurs, barely registering it.

It wasn't long before the doorbell rang for a second time.

"That'll be Faiz," said Nakeisha.

Jacob opened the door. Faizal immediately dived inside out of the pelting downpour. He had only come from a little further up the street but the rain must have lashed at him the whole way. He dripped all over the rug.

"Oh man, look at these new trainers! Flippin' weather!

6

Tried to jump that massive puddle by your front gate but didn't make it, did I?" Faizal stopped by the mirror in the hallway to smooth his jet-black hair back into place before wandering into the kitchen to join Nakeisha. Jacob followed again.

"That game won't have saved properly," Faizal said, shaking his head.

"Honestly, you two! You're more alike than you think," laughed Nakeisha.

"Did you see the lightning, though?" Faizal asked. "I think it hit the top of the headland, you know."

"I once read that a lightning bolt can contain a billion volts of electricity," Jacob offered.

"It might have taken out a tree!" Faizal continued.

"Nah, I think it hit the side of the cliff. Maybe we should check it out," Nakeisha suggested.

Jacob thought of the coastline of their village, which curved around the edge of the bay. He wondered if the lightning could have caused any damage to the rocks by the sea. The area was known to visitors as the

Jurassic Coast, but Jacob knew that the local geology contained just as much history from the Triassic and Cretaceous periods, too. No one seemed to mention those as much.

"I ain't going back out there in a hurry," Faizal was saying.

"Oh, come on, you two. It's only a bit of rain. You won't dissolve," Nakeisha pleaded.

Jacob pictured himself and his friends rushing around the beach like zombies as the falling rain started to dissolve them. *People don't dissolve*, he reassured himself. *It's rocks and soil that are eroded by the rain and wind, not us.*

"Actually, it might make for good fossil-hunting conditions after the storm passes," he suggested. Neither of his friends seemed to hear him, though. Nakeisha was teasing Faizal about the amount of excess hair gel that might wash down his face if they were to go outside again.

The doorbell rang for the third time.

"What's going on here today?" called Jacob's mum

from the lounge. "It's like Piccadilly Circus."

Jacob opened the door to let in Gabi, thinking that the famous Piccadilly Circus in London was not very busy if it only had three or four people passing through.

"I knew you would all be here," Gabi announced as she plodded in to join the others. "How come you're not in the den? Have you raided that new stronghold yet? Oh, and did you see the lightning?"

Nakeisha filled her in on how they had carried out their raid and found new gems and weapons, then the power had gone off around the same time as the lightning and they'd probably need to do it all over again. "How are you, anyway, Gabs? Everything OK with the check-up?" she asked.

"Oh, you know. Still just feeling tired and worn out easily. Got another appointment in a couple of weeks. Hey, let's go up to the den! I've got something cool to tell you – something really weird happened out there," Gabi said.

Intrigued, they dashed upstairs after her, Jacob being the last into his own den. Nakeisha crashed onto the sofa bed and Faizal spun round in the swivel chair at the desk. Jacob sat on his beanbag as Gabi held court in the middle of the room. He worried about her sometimes, always feeling easily exhausted, but he admired her positivity, too.

"I swear that this is true," she began.

Faizal groaned and played with the spinning globe on the desk.

"Honestly, guys," Gabi continued. "We were just in the car, coming back down the main road into the village. We saw the lightning come down from the sky. You can ask my stepmum if you don't believe me. It zapped somewhere into the side of the cliff in the bay."

"Told you!" shouted Nakeisha.

"Yeah, but that's not all," said Gabi. "Afterwards, you could see this weird light coming from near where it had struck. For a few seconds, it was like the cliffside was glowing or something. I'm telling you, it was really strange."

The group looked at one another. Jacob eyed Gabi suspiciously, thinking that lightning couldn't make rocks glow. *But then*, he pondered, *if it did contain a billion volts of electricity...*

"See? We should check it out!" Nakeisha repeated. She jumped up from the sofa bed and looked out through the window. "The rain is definitely stopping. I can see some blue sky through the clouds now."

Faizal covered his face with his hands and groaned even louder. He swivelled round to turn his back on the others, giving the globe one more spin.

"Jacob, you up for it?" Gabi looked him in the eye.

Jacob considered whether he was being pushed for the casting vote. He couldn't quite tell what Gabi's stare was supposed to mean. He didn't want to upset anyone. He thought it highly unlikely that they would see any glowing rocks or frazzled trees. However, there might be some fresh ammonites washed up on the beach or unusual shells uncovered for his collection.

"Those clouds *are* clearing," he said, motioning towards the window, "and if the power's off everywhere, we can't do much inside. We may as well go out for a bit."

"Ugh. Fine!" said Faizal, as it became clear that he was out-voted.

Chapter Two

By the time they were heading out of the door, the rain had eased to a misty drizzle. Jacob had stuffed some useful supplies into his rucksack, as usual. He had his hand lens, his binoculars and a miniature hammer, among other tools. He never went to the beach – or anywhere, in fact – without his bag.

Faizal shook out the wet raincoat that he'd arrived in earlier. He had reluctantly borrowed wellies from Jacob, taking off his white trainers and placing them neatly next to each other in the hall. Pulling on the boots, he tucked in his expensive tracksuit bottoms, complaining that they had better not get dirty. "It's gonna be muddy, you know," he had warned them several times.

With everyone decked out in coats and hats, they headed down the road to the main part of the village. From there, they could take the cliff steps down onto the beach. It was fairly quiet at this time of the year; seaside visitors were few and far between during the winter months. The whole place was a different sight compared with the hustle and bustle when the summer tourists arrived again.

They reached the crumbling Jurassic Coastal Museum, which looked as old as some of the exhibits inside it. Jacob loved learning about the displays it housed but, for some reason, he always found the place creepy-looking. Maybe it was something about the stained, old stone, or maybe the dark green moss that spread from every crack. It just did not seem welcoming.

Nakeisha was the first to spot Sam outside. He was in their class at school.

Sam was sitting on a bench outside the museum kicking the toe of his dirty old boots into the ground. He jumped up hopefully when he saw the others and pushed his glasses up the bridge of his nose.

"Hey – where are you guys going?" he asked, peering out from under a long, messy fringe of hair.

"Nowhere," said Faizal and Gabi at exactly the same time. "Jinx!" They both looked at each other and giggled.

Sam bowed his head.

"Just down to the beach –" Jacob began.

"You've probably got stuff to do and we're in a hurry," Faizal butted in.

"Yeah, come on, before it rains again," Gabi agreed and tugged on Nakeisha's arm as she followed Faizal's lead.

Nakeisha tagged along but looked back at Sam, pulling an apologetic face. Sam dug his hands into the pockets of his scruffy-looking jeans, then sat back down. Jacob saw him watching their group disappear through the community gardens and around the corner towards the steep cliff steps.

"Why don't you like him?" Nakeisha asked when they were out of earshot.

"Well, one – he's such a loner; two – he pokes his nose in..." Faizal began, counting out the points on his fingers for effect.

"...and three – he's just weird," added Gabi. "He's always hanging around the museum... or sneaking up on people... or lurking near those fossil-hunting tourist tours that old Mister Penniket runs..."

"Oh, yeah. That guy creeps me out, too. I heard that he keeps dead animals in his flat above the museum," Faizal said, adding a mock shiver.

"Exactly. I heard that he kills them and wears their skins. Why would anyone want to hang around near him?" Gabi said.

Jacob adjusted his shoulders uncomfortably under his rucksack. Admittedly, it annoyed him that Mister Penniket brought summer tourist groups trampling over the beach and taking the fossils that they knew nothing about. He thought about Faizal and Gabi's words but didn't reply. Nakeisha caught his eye and shrugged.

*

After negotiating the steps and a stretch of sodden beach, they neared the spot that Gabi had described. The jagged cliffs rose up from the beach. Wild grass at the top extended down the crags in haphazard places; other parts of the cliff were bare and crumbling. At the base, there were piles of loose rocks to clamber over.

Occasionally, overhanging ledges obscured crevices and even small caves.

"Look at those layers of sedimentary rock," Jacob enthused. "Isn't it amazing how you can see them built up over millions of years?"

"Hey, Jacob. D'you know that you sound like one of Mrs Green's science lessons?" Faizal teased.

"Never mind that," Gabi interrupted. "Look over there!"

She pointed to where the bottom of the cliffs met the ground a little further ahead. More rocks scattered the sand, spreading out from the base as though they'd just been dumped there from a great height.

All four gazed at a large lump of rock that had been detached from the cliffside. The roughly spherical boulder contained a large crack running downwards; it looked like an upturned jacket potato that had split apart. From inside came an eerie, purple glow.

"That is not normal," said Jacob, the first to speak.

"*Told* you it had glowed," Gabi beamed, a mixture of smugness and excitement on her face as she started to tell them all about the conversation she and her stepmum had had about the lightning.

"It's not just glowing. Listen," said Nakeisha. "Can you hear that kind of buzzing sound?"

Jacob stared at the source of the strange light. He could hear it, too. If he hadn't known any better, he would have agreed that the rock seemed to be vibrating – but it couldn't be, surely...

"Come on then," Gabi encouraged them. "Let's get a closer look." She didn't wait for anyone's permission. She was already bounding over the straggling rocks towards her destination.

"Take it easy, Gabs," warned Nakeisha.

"Hey – anyone noticing a burning smell?" Faizal asked. He was now at the back of the group, crossing his arms, not moving any closer.

"Yeah – smells like when my mum burns the toast," Nakeisha replied, trying to keep up with Gabi but looking back over her shoulder. "Are you not coming?"

"Looks a bit slippy," Faizal observed. "I might just

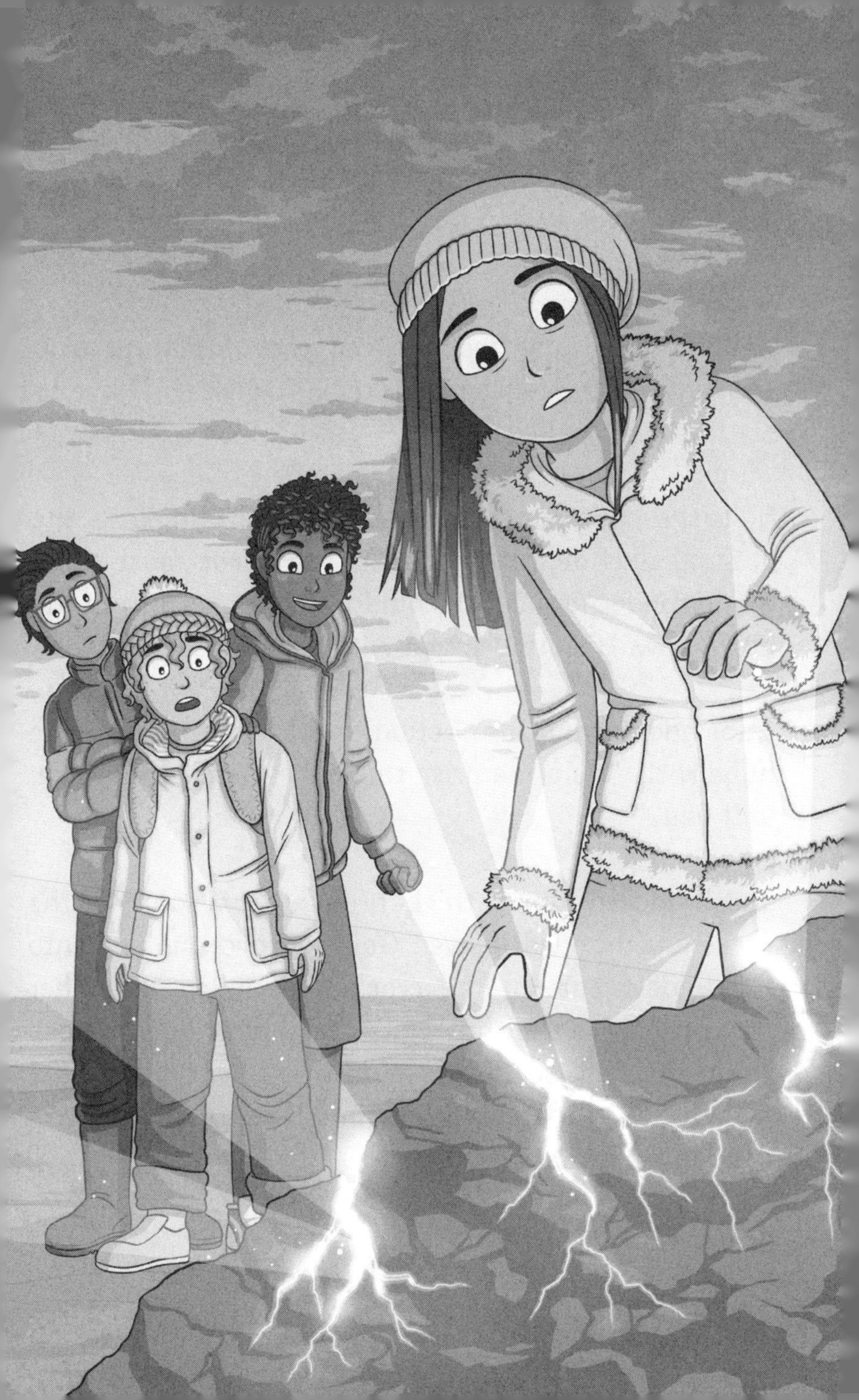

hang on here and keep a lookout. I think I've splashed wet sand up the back of these trackie bottoms, you know." He was twisting to look back at them over his own shoulder.

Gabi had already reached the rock face and was peering into the mysterious crack. "Guys, you have to see this!" she called.

Nakeisha caught up, followed by Jacob. Up close, the buzzing was definitely louder. The burnt toast smell was stronger and Jacob could feel a warmth from the hazy glow. His mind fizzed with questions.

Gabi had sprung into action and leapt up beside the huge rock. "Help me prise this apart. Grab that stick, will you?"

Jacob picked up a thick branch from among the rocks and handed it over. Gabi wedged one end into the widest part of the crack and pulled the other towards her. Nakeisha realised the plan and stepped from one rock to the next until she was beside her friend. Gabi counted to three and the girls pulled with all their might.

Snap!

The branch broke in two and they both staggered backwards. Gabi lost her balance and landed on her backside with a thud.

"Um, you know, you have a wet patch on your bum, now," Faizal offered from a distance.

"You OK?" asked Jacob. Gabi breathed hard and rubbed her temple. She winced as she got to her feet. Knocking wet sand off herself, she scanned the ground for a new tool.

"Yeah, I'm OK, thanks, Jay. Did you bring your fossil hammer? Faizal! Are you gonna help us to see what this thing is or just stand over there like a turnip?"

Jacob rifled in his bag for the hammer. He chuckled as he analysed Gabi's insult and imagined Faizal planted in the ground like a turnip. Maybe Faizal was shamed into action because he was soon stepping cautiously over the rocks, carrying another, thicker branch. He held it out between his thumb and fingertips as though it were contagious.

"Nice one!" said Nakeisha as Faizal reached close enough to pass it on. Gabi wrapped her palm around the middle of the branch and, holding it like a javelin,

21

wedged it into the crack.

This time, Jacob joined in as the girls pulled back on the end of the branch. He felt the rock move a little.

"Tap on the other side of the rock," he told Faizal, handing him the small hammer.

Faizal pulled his sleeves over his hands to cover them. He leaned on the rock on the other side of the crack and gave it a series of whacks with the tool. Gabi counted to three and then, with Nakeisha and Jacob, pulled back again on the branch.

Crack!

This time, it wasn't the wood that gave way – it was the rock.

Chapter Three

Jacob had found many tiny fossils before, living, as they did, in a place where it was so common for them to be uncovered by the elements. However, those were usually just small ammonites or belemnites. His favourite was a perfectly spiralling mollusc shell that sat on the bottom shelf in his den. All of his previous discoveries were no bigger than the palm of his hand. He had dreamed of finding something greater, like the famous fossilist Mary Anning had. She had lived on the same stretch of coast, two hundred years ago. He loved reading about her life and work.

What appeared before them right now, though, was way more incredible than anything Mary had ever discovered – maybe more incredible than *anyone* had ever discovered. This was not just a tooth or a bone, nor was it just an impression in rock or some hard-to-identify remains.

One half of the now-broken rock lay on the ground like a cracked Easter egg. Pressed into the inside of the other half was the full skeleton of some kind of ancient creature.

For a moment, Jacob, Nakeisha and Gabi stood and stared. Behind them, Faizal inched slowly backwards.

"What. Is. That?" he gasped, peering over the shoulders of his friends.

The skull atop the skeleton was about the size of a dog's head. Instead of a snout, however, it looked like it had a large, flat beak.

"Is it real?" asked Gabi.

A few thick, short neck bones connected the creature's head to its body. A full ribcage of bones was curving outwards from the stone. Rising above were longer, thinner bones, which looked like they could have formed wings in full flight.

"I've never seen anything like it," said Nakeisha. Her eyes followed the skeleton along to the tip of its long, raptor-like tail. Two short legs stuck out below the body as if it had frozen in time while out for a walk.

The vibrating sound had not gone away. Jacob wanted to bang his hand against his own head to stop it buzzing inside him. The purple glow had turned to a shroud of mist. It seemed to be growing thicker and soon, they were peering through a dense fog. The burning smell suddenly seemed stronger, too, as though they were breathing in toxic fumes.

"Guys," Jacob coughed, "there's something happening."

Faizal stepped further back. Nakeisha and Gabi held on to each other. Jacob was frozen with fear but, at the same time, fascinated and intrigued enough to want a closer look. He squinted through the swirling purple mist.

"Am I going crazy or is that thing moving?" asked Faizal. There was a slight tremble in his voice.

"It's moving," Jacob confirmed, mesmerised. He covered his nose and mouth to keep out the worsening stench. It was like a triple dose of the stink bombs from the joke shop in town.

The haze surrounding the rock made it hard to see clearly at first, but then it began to thin and clear.

At first, the creature was prising its head away from the rock – not just a skull any more but a head. It was furry – or perhaps feathery. It blinked one golf-ball eye and slowly stretched open its beak in a wide yawn.

Soon, the entire body was wriggling free from where it had been encased. Where the ribs had already been sticking out from the rock, the body now seemed even bulkier. A furry outer layer crept over the bones as they watched. One bony wing – now with fleshy skin stretched across it – popped free from the rock, then a second wing.

Last were the tail, legs and feet. The creature peeled itself away from its stone shell. Gradually, it had become unstuck. Gradually, it had become an actual creature again.

It placed one clawed foot forward onto the rocky ground... then the other... then fell in a clumsy heap, beak first onto the sand.

Faizal let out a squeal. Gabi gave a little snort of laughter at the strange sight. The creature gave a squawk, looked at the four humans and blinked its bulgy eyes.

"O.M.G.," breathed Gabi. "This is amazing. Did that really just happen? Did you lot *see* that?"

"We've set it free from the rock," said Nakeisha.

"I think we've brought the fossil back to life," suggested Faizal. "This is even cooler than anything on *Raider's Peril*."

"Maybe it was to do with the storm," Gabi offered. "Maybe the lightning strike has somehow caused this."

"Caused what, though?" asked Jacob. "What exactly has happened here? I don't understand. This thing looks prehistoric. Now, it's walking around in front of us."

"I dunno about walking. Seems like it can barely stand up!"

Faizal was right. The creature shifted its weight awkwardly from one clawed foot to the other. Each time, it seemed ready to topple over. It turned and looked at the assembled group, tilting its head one way, then the other. Feathery tufts jutted from the back of its neck. It looked confused.

After a little shuffling, it plonked itself down on the sand. Jacob wondered if it had just got tired of trying to stay upright. It almost gave a sigh as it sagged to the floor, and its neck drooped.

"Maybe it's just a baby if it can't walk properly. Look, it has cute fluffy tufts on its front like a baby penguin. Do you think it's friendly?" Nakeisha pondered aloud.

"I don't think it has the energy to attack us, even if it wanted to. I'm going to try stroking it," said Gabi.

"Be careful," warned Jacob.

She crept cautiously towards it. The creature observed her warily. When she was close enough, she reached out her hand in slow motion. The whole time, she was pursing her lips and making soft cooing sounds.

With her first touch, the creature jerked its head a little. Gabi persevered and stroked the back of its neck. After a few seconds, the creature angled its head towards her and produced a throaty, warbling sound. Jacob thought that it sounded like a cat purring.

"I think it likes you," he said, before noticing the rock behind. "Wow! It's left a fossilised impression behind!"

The inside of the boulder now contained a perfectly preserved mould of the creature's skeleton, as though it had been pressed into modelling clay.

"You must know what type of creature it is, Jay. Don't you always know about this kind of thing?" asked Faizal.

"Not this! This is different to anything else *ever*! It's a bit like an Anchiornis, but the legs are too short. It's similar to a Geminiraptor, but with more of a beak. It's like... like a dodo's prehistoric cousin or something!"

"I thought Mrs Green said that dodos were only ever found on some faraway island before they became extinct," Nakeisha said.

"I'm not saying it *is* a dodo. Anyway, they were alive way more recently than dinosaurs – and there are not thought to be any known similar-looking creatures," Jacob replied.

"Yet here we are," said Faizal, gesturing towards the waddling, wobbling, warbling oddity in front of them. The creature cocked its head and squawked, as if in some kind of agreement.

"So, what do we do with it? Should we just leave it here?" said Nakeisha.

"No! It might not survive! Let's keep it as a pet," Gabi blurted out.

"Don't be daft," said Faizal. "Where would it live? How would you look after it? There's no way my dad would let me bring it into the house!"

"I don't think any of us can keep it," said Jacob solemnly. "Maybe we should report it to the RSPCA."

"What would they do?" asked Gabi. "It's not hurt or in danger, and that might draw too much attention to it."

"Yeah – imagine what old Mister Penniket would say! He'd love to get his hands on it," said Nakeisha darkly.

"He'd want it for the museum for sure! Probably put it in a glass case."

"More like skin it alive!" said Faizal.

"I'm telling you – there's no way it's going in that weird museum."

"Then, I guess we need another plan," said Nakeisha.

The creature sat comfortably on the ground between them, taking in its new surroundings. It pecked at the sand, cocked its head at the seagulls flying above and blinked brightly up at them all.

Chapter Four

"Right," said Gabi, after some discussion among the group. She took a couple of deep breaths and rubbed her head. "We're all going to head back along the beach. Keep to the edge where the sand meets the cliffs, because the tide is on its way in. Let's see if she will follow us. Agreed?"

"She?" asked Jacob.

"Yeah, I reckon it's a girl," she shrugged.

"How can we get her to follow us, though?" asked Nakeisha. "We could try offering her some food, I suppose. I bet she's hungry if she's been set in stone for thousands of years."

"Millions, more likely," Jacob corrected her.

"Good idea. What do you think *she* eats, though?" asked Faizal.

"One way to find out," said Gabi. She marched over to the base of the cliff and started pulling at clumps of wet grass. The others watched as she tramped back towards them, a fistful of grass in her right hand. Nearing the creature, she crouched and spoke softly, holding out her grass-filled palm.

"Here's some nice grass. Come on," she cooed.

The creature looked at Gabi inquisitively. It jerked its head from side to side. It looked down at her hand. There was a moment of pause.

Suddenly, it snapped its beak at the grass on Gabi's palm. Snap-snap-snapping away, it flung the grass up in the air in all directions. Gabi fell backwards, giggling.

"I don't think that went down too well," laughed Nakeisha.

"What about some seaweed?" Jacob suggested. He picked some up and dangled it in front of the creature. It was greeted with disinterest. Nakeisha grabbed it and flung it towards Faizal instead.

"Ugh! What did you do that for? It nearly touched

me!" Faizal shrieked. Then, his face lit up. "Hang on. I've got one of these!" He pulled out a squashed-looking cereal bar from his pocket.

Unwrapping one end, he held the snack out at arm's length towards the creature, which craned its feathery neck towards it. *Was it sniffing?* Jacob wondered. *Was it able to sniff?* As he pondered, the creature showed what it thought of Faizal's offering. It gave a loud squawk and rose up, batted its wings and stamped its feet, then turned around and looked out towards the sea instead.

"Pretty sure that prehistoric creatures didn't eat cereal bars," Jacob said.

"Worth a try," Faizal replied. "I don't remember seeing any books on your shelf telling you what to feed a fossil creature that comes back to life after millions of years."

That was a fair point, Jacob supposed.

"If we can get her to follow us, there'll be more stuff to try nearer the village," said Gabi. "There might be some fishing bait around the harbour, or we could try things from home, or we could..."

She continued to come up with ideas as they discussed the possibility of returning to the village with their discovery. The spot where they had found the creature was slightly sheltered from view on either side by the shape of the cliffs. The village would be much riskier.

"What if someone sees us? What if Mister Penniket is out near the museum?" asked Faizal.

"He's right," agreed Nakeisha. "We do need to be careful until we decide what to do with her."

"We don't even know if it will follow us yet, anyway," Jacob pointed out. "It might fly away. It might not want to move at all."

"Let's see," said Gabi. She started to back slowly away, still facing the creature. She tapped on her thighs. "Come on," she beckoned softly. She edged back a little further and called the creature again.

It looked at her and shuffled slightly.

"She's moving," whispered Nakeisha. She tiptoed to Gabi's side and joined in with the beckoning. "Here, flappy girl," she sang as they both tapped their legs gently.

The creature shuffled a little more on the spot. Then it placed one foot forward.

"She's definitely moving!" cried Nakeisha.

Jacob and Faizal joined in. All four friends stood in a row, bending their knees slightly, patting their thighs and making strange cooing noises.

"We must look flippin' ridiculous," said Faizal.

Nevertheless, he carried on. Inching along, the creature began to follow unsteadily. Little by little, they all moved along, separated by a few feet of wet sand.

Then, from high in the sky above, a seagull swooped down. It flew low along the beach, cawing loudly, before perching on the side of the cliff. Startled, the creature stopped and watched. It looked up longingly and gave a feeble squawk back of its own.

"She looks sad, now," said Gabi.

The seagull set off again in flight. The fossil creature watched, then stretched its own wings with a half-hearted flap. It hopped into the air but barely left the ground.

"I think it's trying to fly," said Jacob.

"I don't want her to fly away," said Gabi. "I want to look after her!"

"You might not have to worry about the flying," said Faizal doubtfully. They looked on as the creature flapped and hopped again, failing miserably to produce anything that resembled flight.

"She's not following us any more, though," Gabi moaned.

"I've got an idea!" Jacob announced suddenly. He took off his rucksack and placed it on the ground. After a quick rummage around, he triumphantly held up what he'd been looking for.

"A torch?" said Nakeisha. "But it's the afternoon. It's not even dark."

Despite the daylight, the storm had left behind a dull, cloudy sky. Jacob hoped that it was gloomy enough for his idea to work. He pointed the torch down at the dark, damp sand near their feet and flicked it on.

The light hitting the ground was dim but noticeable. Slowly, Jacob raised the torch so that it shone along

the beach onto the sand where the creature stood. The further away he shone it, however, the more the light faded. The creature didn't even notice it.

"Try again!" said Faizal, recognising the plan.

Again, Jacob pointed the torch down near their feet and gradually teased the light along the beach towards the creature, which was gazing casually around at more passing seagulls. On the third attempt, it suddenly snapped its head in the direction of the light. Two wide eyes focused on the ground ahead, it lunged forwards like a cat pouncing on a mouse. It stopped and looked around to see where its prey had gone; as soon as it spotted Jacob's light on the ground, it hopped towards it again.

"Yes! It's working," called Gabi as the creature began to close the gap between them. The group stepped backwards as Jacob continued to tempt it forwards with his torchlight.

"She thinks she's going to catch it," chuckled Nakeisha.

They laughed and took turns flicking the torch on and off, moving it nearer to the creature then jerking it away again. Each time, it hopped or jumped forwards

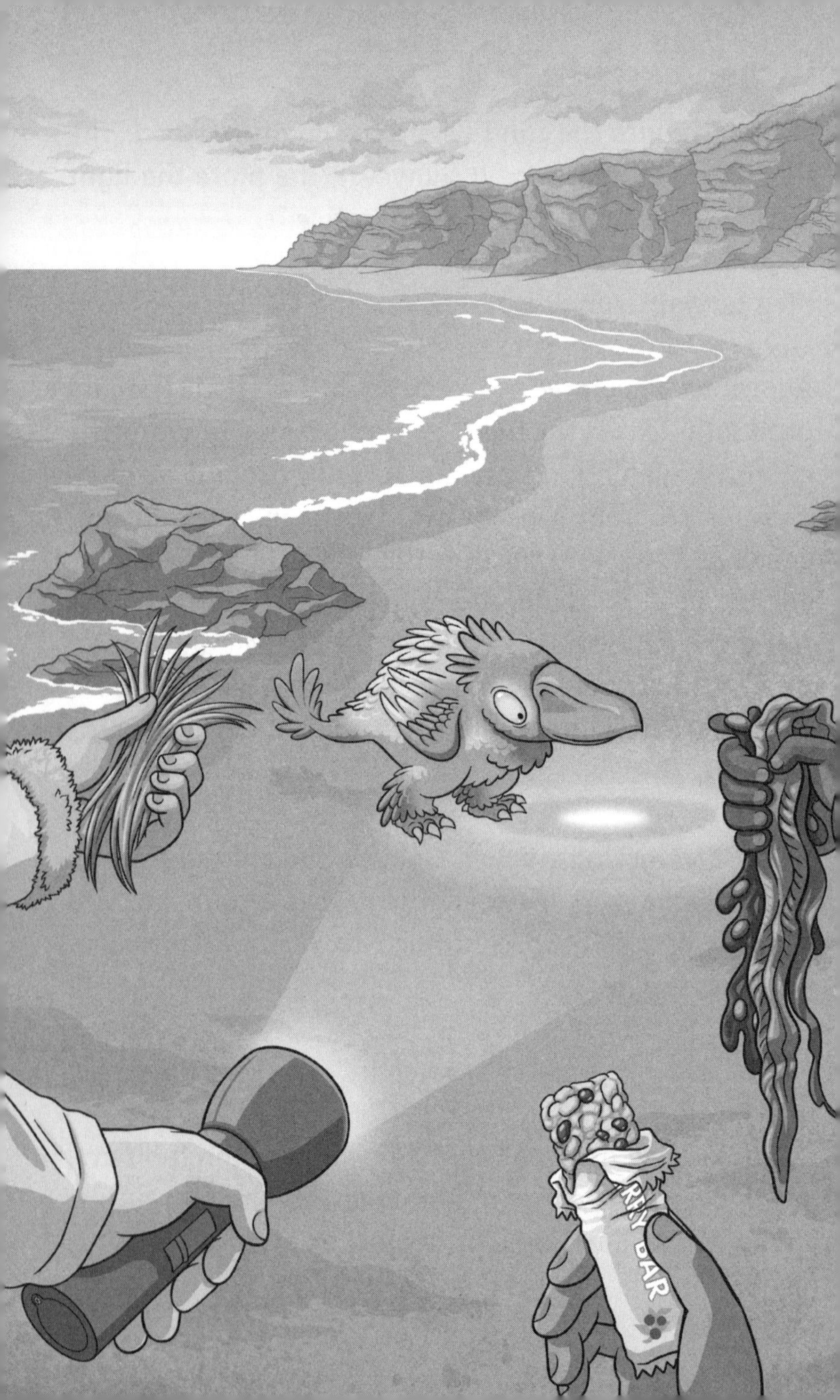

BAR

only to miss out on capturing the elusive prey.

Before long, they realised that they had rounded another section of rocks and were no longer sheltered by the cliffside. Ahead, the open beach stretched towards the steep steps to the village.

"What now?" asked Nakeisha. "We'll get spotted if we go much further."

"Mister Penniket is bound to be out somewhere," added Gabi.

"It doesn't even need to be him. If anyone sees us with this, we'll have blown it. They'll whisk her away in no time," said Faizal.

Jacob smiled. "I think I have another idea."

Chapter Five

Jacob had explained his plan thoroughly.

The girls stayed where they were with the creature. Gabi said that she wasn't sure if she'd have the energy to run, and Nakeisha offered to stay with her. Faizal and Jacob set off running along the beach. They reached the steps leading back up to the community gardens and then steadied their pace.

"What d'you reckon that thing is, then?" Faizal asked, panting as they climbed the steps.

"I have no idea," Jacob replied, equally out of breath. "I've never seen anything like it. Even if it had turned out to be just a fossil, it would have been amazing – but it came back to life before our eyes! It doesn't make any sense."

"Yeah, it's pretty cool that we found it," Faizal agreed as they rounded the top of the steps back into the gardens.

"Found what?" came an unexpected voice.

"S-S-Sam!" Jacob gasped. Neither of them had noticed that the boy was still lurking near the bench where they had last seen him. *How much did he just hear?* Jacob wondered in a momentary panic.

"Nothing," Faizal responded. Jacob cast a cautionary look over his shoulder, back down towards the beach. Sam seemed to follow his gaze.

"We're just heading back to Faizal's house for a bit," Jacob said, trying to make his lie as close to the truth as he could.

"Where are the girls? You were with Gabi and Nakeisha earlier," Sam quizzed.

"Uh... they had something else to do," said Faizal. "Come on, Jay. We need to get back to do that thing." He tugged Jacob's arm and widened his eyes.

At first, Jacob wondered what was wrong with him. Then, he understood what Faizal's wide eyes meant. It was like that time when he had tried to stop Jacob from reminding Mrs Green they hadn't been given their spelling homework. It meant: *stop talking and get moving!*

They both headed off, away from Sam. When they were just about to round the corner at the opposite side of the gardens, Jacob looked back. He saw Sam giving them one last glance before turning in the direction of the steps to the beach.

"He's going down there," Jacob whispered urgently to Faizal.

"Told you – he's so flippin' nosy. If he finds out where the girls are, he'll be telling everyone about the creature – probably old Mister Penniket, too. We need to hurry up if we're going to get back to them in time."

The boys passed the coastal museum and ran up the hill. Through one of the museum's grimy windows, a bearded, weather-beaten face watched them go.

*

As quickly as they could, they dashed into Faizal's house. Faizal grabbed a fancy-looking dog coat belonging to his pet poodle, Alfie. The coat had a white fur collar; the rest of it was a red tartan design, like a Scottish kilt. Wrapped around it was Alfie's extendable lead with a collar and harness. Faizal passed them behind his back to Jacob, to stuff into the rucksack. At the same time, he shouted into the lounge to his dad's girlfriend, who didn't look round from watching TV.

"Hi, Vicky. Just forgot something. Going back down to the beach with Jacob. Is that OK?"

"Yes, but be back for when your dad gets home," came the reply.

Faizal and Jacob were soon back out of the house and hurrying down the hill the way they had come – towards the village, past the museum and turning through the gardens before finally hurtling down the steps to the beach. Just when they thought that there was no sign of Sam poking his nose in, he appeared at the bottom of the steps.

"Oh, you're like a bad smell," Faizal said to him. "You

always seem to be hanging around."

Sam looked at Jacob. Jacob knew that it was a mean thing for Faizal to have said. *Should he stick up for Sam even though Faizal was his friend?*

Before he was able to decide, Sam spoke instead. Turning away from Jacob with a look of disappointment, he fixed his eyes on Faizal.

"I've seen what you found," he said.

Sam's words exploded between the three of them like silent fireworks. Jacob felt the air fizz with a charge of energy. Faizal clenched his fists.

Jacob tried to muster the words to help the situation. *Ask Sam to keep quiet? Pretend they didn't know what he was talking about?*

His thoughts didn't catch up in time. Sam cast his eyes from Faizal back to Jacob again. Then the boy ran up the steps, taking them two at a time. Faizal turned as if to follow but Jacob stopped him.

"We need to get to the girls and find out what happened," Jacob said.

"What if he tells everyone, though? You heard what he said. He'll have half the village down here – probably old Mister Penniket, too. They'll whisk the creature away to a museum or a science lab or something."

"Then, it's even more important for us to get back to it first," Jacob reasoned.

Faizal was finally persuaded and the pair set off, quicker than ever, along the sand. When they reached the area where they had left Gabi and Nakeisha, the girls were nowhere to be seen.

"They were supposed to wait for us here, where they were out of sight," said Jacob.

"I know but that flippin' meddler, Sam, obviously found them. They might have gone to try and catch us up," Faizal answered.

"No, we'd have seen them," Jacob countered. "We couldn't have missed them, the way we came. Plus, they've got a walking, squawking fossil in tow."

"Then, where are they?" Faizal asked, spinning his head from one side to the other and searching the empty beach around them.

"Maybe Sam frightened the creature away," Jacob suggested.

The pair stood and looked around. To their right, the sweeping curve of the cliffs led back towards the steps to the village. In the opposite direction, to their left, the steep cliff sides became more irregular, creating nooks and caves that were blocked from view. Further along that way was where they had discovered the creature. The strip of sand was narrower than earlier due to the incoming tide. The waves of the English Channel stretched to infinity in the distance. Behind them, the cliffs rose up to the sky.

A faint whistle travelled through the air from behind them. Both boys' heads snapped round and looked up in the direction of the noise. Jacob scanned the gradual slope. Tufts of grass jutted out from bare sandstone. Other sections were covered in green. The trees at the top looked so far away, they were like a row of broccoli.

Hidden in one patch of undergrowth, less than halfway up the slope, he spotted a head popping up, then another: Gabi and Nakeisha. Gabi whistled again. Jacob pointed them out to Faizal, who was still turning left and right, looking for the source of the noise.

"What are you doing up there?" Faizal called.

"Is it safe to come back down?" Gabi shouted in reply. She cupped her hands around either side of her mouth and emerged further into view.

"Safe from what?" asked Jacob.

"Is the coast clear? Has Sam gone?" called Nakeisha.

"Yes, but he knows all about the creature," said Faizal.

"No, he doesn't," Gabi chimed in as she carefully started to edge her way back down the slope of the cliff, leaving Nakeisha behind. When she reached the bottom, she began to fill the boys in on what had happened.

The girls had spotted Sam walking along the beach in their direction. Before he could see them or the creature, they had led it as quickly as they could up the cliff to their precarious hiding place.

"Sam walked right past, below where we were hiding. He never even noticed us!" Gabi beamed. "He went back again not long afterwards and still never thought to look up at where we were."

"I can't believe you managed to stay out of sight and not be noticed," Faizal enthused, "but hang on a minute – where's that thing actually gone?"

"I thought you'd never ask," Gabi said with a smug grin. "Check this out!"

She called up to Nakeisha, who had been holding on to their new fossil friend in anticipation. Once Nakeisha let it go, Gabi started to wave and call out. It came waddling into sight halfway up the cliff, trying to keep its balance on the slope, on two unsteady legs. Then, with a flap of its wings, it made a half-jumping, half-flying kind of leap. Skidding and bouncing in a zigzag down the cliffside, it reached the beach in an untidy, sandy bundle. Finally, it shook its fur and announced its arrival near Gabi's feet with a squawk.

"She's getting better at the flying," Gabi announced proudly. "We were just teaching her to flap her wings before we had to hide. And she's totally following us and listening to us, aren't you? Clever girl!" she cooed and gushed.

Jacob and Faizal looked at each other. "Hmm. I think a few more lessons are needed yet, Gabs!" said Faizal with a smirk, as the creature flapped the sand out of its feathers and gave its head a little shake.

Nakeisha was the last to arrive back on the flat of the beach, following the creature's path.

"Did you get the harness and coat?" she asked.

"Yep! And it looks like we need the lead even more if she is finding her wings," said Faizal. "Let's try and get these on her before we risk heading back up to the village again." A hint of fine rain seemed to be blowing through the air once more and the tide was swallowing up the beach rapidly.

"There's just one more thing, though," said Jacob. The other three turned to look at him. "Sam told us that he knew what we'd found. If he didn't actually see you or the creature... what did he see?"

Chapter Six

"We can't stay down here for much longer. Let's try to get the creature back to one of our houses. Then, we can decide what to do with it," Jacob said. He pulled out the dog coat and harness from his rucksack.

"What to do with *her*," Gabi corrected.

"We should give her a name," added Nakeisha, "and then we can make her an avatar in the game and she can be like our guild mascot."

The creature looked at them, cocked its head to one side and then the other, and squawked in agreement.

"Not sure she'd be any good at raiding another guild's stronghold, Keisha... but Jay's right. We need to get it – her – whatever – somewhere we can think," said Faizal. "There's no chance at mine, though. Alfie might only be a poodle but he's got the nose of a bloodhound. He'd sniff out a strange creature in the house in no time."

"I wish she could come to mine but there's no room to hide in our flat," said Nakeisha.

"I wish we could use my place, too, but there are always too many people around at the B&B. It would be too risky," said Gabi.

All three of them looked at Jacob, who was untangling Alfie's lead. When he sensed their gaze, he looked up. He wondered why they were just staring at him.

"What?" he asked, confused.

"Your house, Jacob!" said Faizal, rolling his eyes.

"My house?" he said, his voice rising noticeably higher than usual. "My mum would go mad! I've got Steg and Rex. I've got too much stuff!"

"Yeah, but just think about it," said Faizal. "More stuff means more hiding places. The hamsters mean there's a bit of noise and mess, anyway. Plus, you could do some research on what type of creature it is."

Jacob thought about Faizal's last point. He did like the idea of a real-life project – a fossil creature from history to study. He was itching to look through his books for anything that looked like Phyllis. His mum usually left him to it in the den because she knew that he didn't like anyone moving or tidying his stuff.

"Fine," he said. "Help me get this coat on her and let's get her back to my place before anyone sees us."

"Yay!" smiled Nakeisha, clapping her hands together. "And you called her *'her'*."

Gabi crouched down and began to stroke the back of the creature's head. She made the clucking and cooing noises again as a distraction while, from behind, Faizal prepared the tartan dog coat over the harness. He mouthed a countdown to Jacob –

"Three... two... one..."

 – and then lunged to wrap them around the creature's back and wings. As he held them in place, Jacob grabbed at the straps underneath and quickly clipped them together under the chest.

The creature squawked and hopped. It tried to flap but found its wings fastened to its side under the coat and harness. Cornered against the cliff by the gang of four, it danced around in circles before giving up and looking at them with a mix of confusion and annoyance.

"It's for your own good," said Gabi softly, as she clipped the lead on to the harness. Her reassuring voice seemed to calm the creature. "Now, what are we going to call you?"

The group set off walking.

"Look at how she waddles as she walks," said Nakeisha, looking down at the creature as they ambled along. "She reminds me of my granny and her friend who go shopping together."

"Is your granny's friend the one with the big eyes?" asked Gabi.

Nakeisha laughed. "Yeah. Have you noticed, too? It's like she's always staring at you!"

"That's it, then," said Faizal. "They've got the same big, bulgy eyes; they both waddle when they walk; and they're both really, really old! We need to name her after your granny's friend!"

"What's she called?" asked Jacob.

"Phyllis," said Nakeisha.

They all burst out laughing. "Phyllis the fossil," said Jacob.

"Perfect," said Gabi.

When they reached the bottom of the steps, they knew they had to be on their guard. Jacob and Faizal went up first to see if anyone was around. Gabi guided Phyllis with the lead. The creature hopped up the first couple of steps, following Nakeisha. Faizal headed back down part of the way to shout that the coast was clear. At the top, they gathered together again.

Avoiding the main path through the gardens and the coastal museum would take them away from where they had bumped into Sam so, this time, they decided to take a different route. The other exit from the gardens took them past the back of the arcade and then behind a row of shops, where big metal bins stood with empty cardboard boxes stacked beside them. However, this was risky because anyone could come out of the back of one of the shops.

The alley at the end of the backstreet was in sight when Phyllis pulled on the lead even more than she had been doing already. Gabi struggled to hold on. Beak in the air, Phyllis barrelled into one tower of cardboard boxes, toppling them over and scattering a few bits of rubbish that had been left inside them.

"What is she *doing*?" Gabi moaned. Phyllis still had her head in the boxes, pushing things aside with her beak. Finally, the answer to Gabi's question became clear.

"I think we've found what she eats," said Nakeisha.

Phyllis was gulping down the stinky leftovers from behind the fish and chip shop.

They let her eat for a few moments, staying crowded around her and desperately trying to keep watch.

"We need to keep going," Jacob said eventually. "Someone could come out of a back door any second."

Heading through the alleyway, there was still no sign of anyone around. They skirted the edge of the harbour car park, getting closer to the road leading out of the main village. Two more corners to navigate... then, a voice called out from behind them.

"Hey!"

They turned, keeping Phyllis between them all.

"You've got to be kidding me. Where did you spring from this time?" said Faizal as Sam hurried into view.

"Just walking around. So, you guys are all together again?" Sam replied.

"Yeah. Sorry, Sam. We've got to get back now, though," Nakeisha said. Sam craned his neck to one side then the other, trying to catch a glimpse between them. Jacob made sure that he was blocking the view of Phyllis' head and beak. Gabi was shuffling into position herself, to block her two feathered legs and clawed feet. Faizal was shielding her tail behind his legs, looking wary.

"What's that you have with you?" asked Sam, still angling his head for a better look.

"It's just my dog – not that it's any of your business. We're just walking my dog." Faizal's words were sounding a bit garbled.

"Oh, yeah. I've seen you with your dog in that coat before," Sam replied slowly. "You didn't have the dog with you earlier, though."

"We had the dog with us," Gabi blurted out. She was struggling to keep Phyllis at her feet as the lead strained and the creature wriggled impatiently.

"But I saw all of you earlier. There was no dog..." Sam mused. "Wait! What's wrong with its paws? They look weird."

"No, they don't," Faizal said, defensively. "It's just my dog. He's been on the beach. Always gets things

stuck to him."

Phyllis was still moving and pulling. She bumped the back of Gabi's legs. Gabi bumped into Faizal and tried to cover it like she was doing some kind of weird dance move.

"Hang on – stop moving. Why are you all hiding the dog? I can only see two legs. Where's its other legs?"

Jacob started to sweat. Phyllis let out one of her squawks. Nakeisha coughed loudly in an attempt to cover it up.

"What was that noise?" asked Sam, getting more and more animated.

Faizal whispered to Nakeisha. Then, he stepped forward, closer to Sam, blocking his view even more. "Never mind my dog. What did you mean earlier when you said you 'knew what we had seen'?" he asked.

Nakeisha spotted the cue and turned to run up the hill, grabbing Gabi as she twisted. Gabi followed, understanding the plan. Jacob hovered between running and staying, not really sure why the girls had suddenly bolted. He took a few steps away as Faizal confronted Sam.

"I – I went down the beach, to the rocks in the cove," stammered Sam. He was trying to look past Faizal but the girls were a blur as they dashed out of sight. Gabi tugged Phyllis along on the lead while Nakeisha ran behind, continuing to block Sam's view. "Are you sure that was your dog? Why are they running away?"

"I've told you it's my dog. Now, what do you mean, you 'went to the rocks'?" Faizal persisted. Sam looked squarely at him. Jacob shuffled uncomfortably a few paces away.

"You guys found that rock with the fossil imprint, didn't you? I saw it. The rock had split apart."

Jacob's breath caught in his throat.

"I haven't told anyone about it," said Sam. "If you guys found it, it's your discovery. *You* should, though. It might be important. It's a whole skeleton. It would be amazing for the museum – think of all the tourists who would pay to come and see it!"

It took a few moments for Jacob to piece together the puzzle. By this time, Faizal had already beaten him to the realisation. What Sam had seen was not the creature itself. He had just seen the fossilised imprint in the rock.

"Oh, yeah," Faizal said. "It was the rock. OK... well, you're right. Just, uh, don't tell anyone about it just yet, all right? We've got to catch up with the others." Faizal stepped backwards a few paces as he spoke, keeping his eyes on Sam. He tapped Jacob's arm and nodded his head in the direction of Jacob's house. They turned and ran up the hill after the others.

*

When they reached the front garden, Nakeisha and Gabi were waiting. The boys arrived and Faizal splashed through the puddle by the gate. Phyllis popped her head out from behind the girls and gave a squawk. Tufts of fur on her head and neck stuck up, making it look as if she'd just got out of bed. Her head was being drawn in every direction as she took in the new sights and sounds around her.

Jacob opened the door and ushered them all inside. He checked that his mum wasn't in the hallway, then put his head around the door to the lounge to find her there, still working on her laptop. The others stayed behind him, willing Phyllis to stay quiet.

"Hey, Mum. Is it OK if we go back to up the den?"

"Yes, if your friends don't mind the mess!" came the reply. "The power has come back on if you want to play on your games again."

"Thanks," said Jacob, before closing the lounge door and whispering to the others, "Bring Phyllis quietly!"

They all made their way up the stairs, Phyllis hopping heavily onto each step. When everyone was safely inside the den, Jacob closed the door behind them.

"Phew! That was close. What did Sam say after we'd left?" Gabi asked.

"He doesn't know about Phyllis," Jacob replied. "He thinks we just found the impression fossil."

"Well, that buys us some time," said Gabi. "I'm going to have to go really soon, though. I told my stepmum I'd be back to help with some of the weekend B&B jobs."

"Me too," said Faizal. "My dad will wonder where I

am, once he's home. Now that the power is back on, we can all talk online."

"Right. Let's all meet up again in the morning and we can decide what to do," suggested Nakeisha.

"Wait. W-What? You're all leaving? Meet in the morning?" stammered Jacob. "Where's Phyllis gonna stay overnight?"

The three of them looked back at him, as though the answer were obvious. Faizal opened out his hands to indicate the room they were in.

"Here? Overnight? No one said anything about overnight!" cried Jacob.

They all looked down at Phyllis, who looked back at them, blinking her big, round eyes. She already had some torn paper sticking out one side of her beak. On the floor, Jacob's Mary Anning book was now missing half a page. He flopped backwards onto his beanbag, covering his eyes with his hands.

"This is going to be a long night," he said.

Chapter Seven

After all the others had left, Jacob sat on the beanbag in his den. Phyllis had hopped up onto the desk, sending the globe toppling. They had relieved her of the coat and harness. There wasn't much room to fly in the den but it didn't stop her stretching her wings.

"What actually are you?" Jacob whispered to the creature. She blinked blankly back at him and shuffled her feet, knocking a pencil to the floor.

Jacob picked up one of his dinosaur guides that he'd started leafing through earlier. Nothing in there matched exactly with the thing standing in front of him. Most of the prehistoric creatures were made to look quite mean in the illustrations that appeared in books. He knew that no one knew for certain about the colours and coats of dinosaurs. Phyllis didn't look mean, though – mainly just cute and confused.

He still couldn't believe the events of the day: the lightning and the storm; the cracked-open rock; the fossil that appeared to have come alive in front of his eyes. Now what? Where did this creature belong?

He considered the thought. He couldn't bear the idea of Phyllis being poked and prodded in a science lab and having tests performed on her – even though it would be interesting to find out where she had come from.

The coastal museum was full of fossil finds from the local area. There were huge displays showing the changes in the rocks and cliffs over thousands and millions of years. Jacob was sure that old Mister Penniket would love to get his hands on the creature... but what would he do with her? She couldn't live in a museum.

He thought of the bearded old man and what everyone said about him. Jacob mainly disliked that he took all the tourist groups trampling over the beach, taking the fossils and shells that he'd like to find himself. There were also the rumours, though. If he was an animal killer, then maybe he'd want to stuff Phyllis and put her in a glass case!

His mind had wandered. He looked back at Phyllis, still on the desk. She was looking out of the window, staring at the sky.

66

"I wonder what you're thinking," he mumbled.

Phyllis responded with a sad, gurgling noise. It wasn't a squawk this time; if Jacob hadn't known better, he would have sworn that he had seen Phyllis sigh.

"Maybe you need a drink after your fish supper earlier," he muttered. Slipping out of the door, he dashed to the kitchen and filled a bowl with water.

He wasn't gone long but, when he got back, Phyllis had moved from the desk to the bookshelves opposite, on top of which sat Jacob's hamster cage. She was staying perfectly still with her eyes locked on Steg, who was running inside his wheel.

"Woah there, Phyllis!" he called softly. "Let's not scare Steg or Rex, shall we?"

With difficulty, he picked her up and placed her on the floor next to the bowl of water. She stuck her beak into the bowl then shook her head, splashing water around. Then, she hopped up onto the windowsill and tried to get onto the chest of drawers, despite there being nowhere near enough room. Amid the mess that she was making, she knocked off Jacob's favourite spiral mollusc fossil and chipped the smooth, round edge.

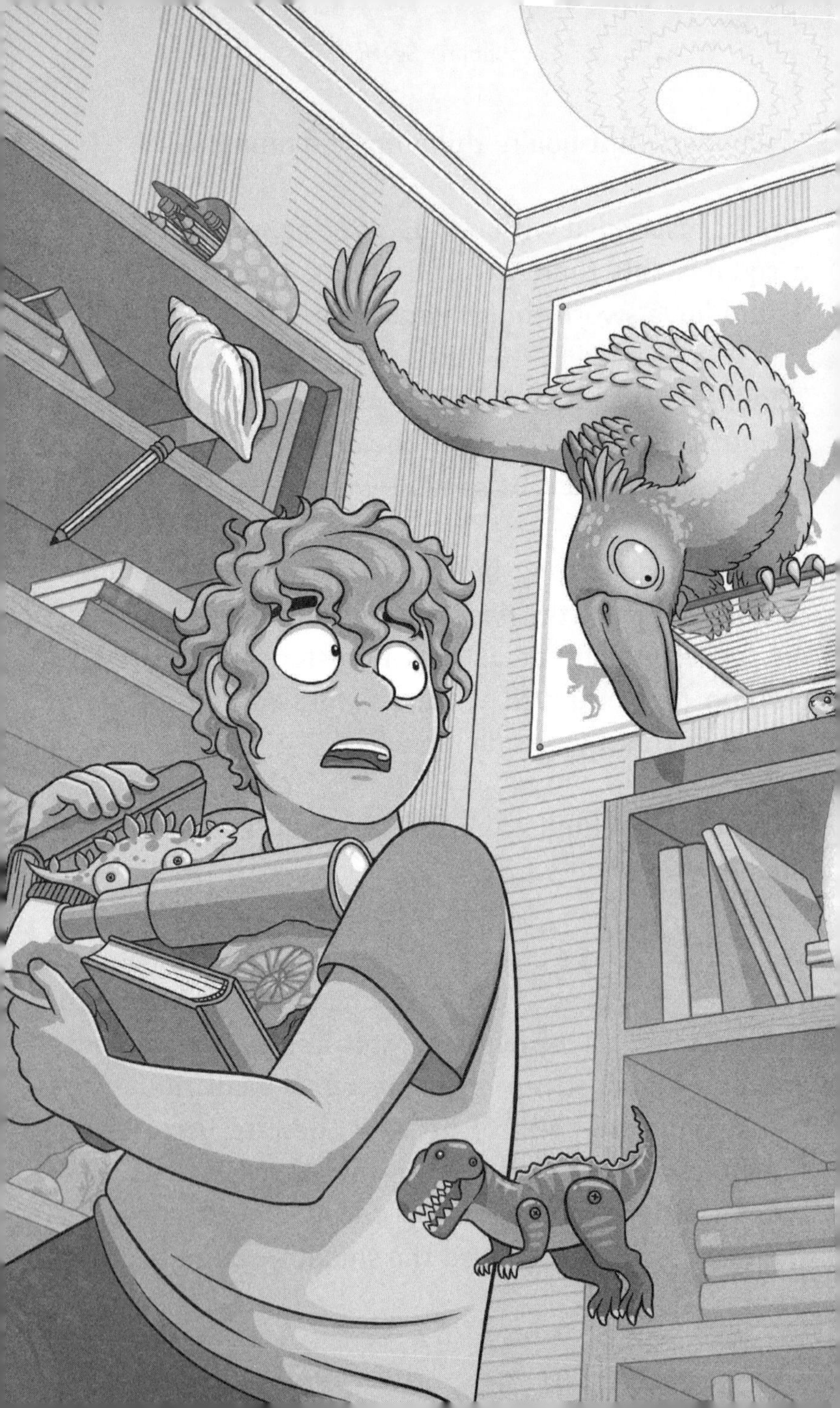

"Agh! Phyllis!" he said through gritted teeth and put his hands to his head again.

The next few hours were spent frustratingly trying to keep Phyllis calm and quiet. Jacob logged on to *Raider's Peril* and told the others about the water, the hamsters and the general destruction of his den.

"It's starting to look more ransacked in here than the stronghold we raided earlier," he said.

The others laughed as if that were a joke. Everyone had some advice and suggestions on what to do. It wasn't the same as them being around to actually help, though.

Jacob asked his mum if he could sleep in the den, as he did sometimes. Meanwhile, Phyllis hopped from desk to drawers to windowsill to shelves until Jacob couldn't cope any longer. He pulled the duvet cover over his head as he sat on the sofa bed and pulled his knees into his chest. He closed his eyes to block out the constant pecking sound. In his mind, Jacob started to list all the dinosaur names he could think of, hoping that it would distract him. Maybe it would remind him of something resembling Phyllis, too.

Pterodactyl – had longer wings and pointy head; Velociraptor – no beak or wings and much meaner-looking; Anchiornis...

*

"Morning, sleepy head! Are you awake yet?"

Jacob stirred, hearing his mum's voice. He opened one eye and peered out from under the duvet. He saw her poking her head around the door. After he chose not to respond, he felt her giving his toes a wiggle before disappearing again.

His mind felt a bit foggy. With a yawn and a stretch, he peeled open a second groggy eyelid. In his brain, strange events and images bounced around. The first thought that clearly formed was that he had slept in the den. That was not unusual, though the sofa bed was not as comfortable as his actual bed and he felt a little ache in his back. Immediately after that thought, however, came the memory of *why* he had slept on the sofa bed this particular time.

"Phyllis!" he shouted, jumping up.

"What did you say?" called his mum from out on the

landing somewhere.

"Um... nothing, Mum. Just getting up. I'm OK. I didn't say anything. I mean, I didn't mean to... I'll be down in a minute!"

"Right. Well, you need to think about tidying up that den afterwards. It's worse than ever!"

Frantically, he scanned the room. He had fallen asleep and slept all night. His mum had just wandered in. Where was Phyllis? Surely, Mum had not seen her, or she would have probably screamed! If Mum hadn't seen Phyllis – and he couldn't see the creature now – then where was she?

He threw the duvet off the sofa bed – no sign there.

He crawled under the desk (and found the missing tripod leg which had meant that his telescope had not been able to stand up for weeks) – but no sign of Phyllis there, either. His headset hung off the side of the chair with some foam spilling out of the inside. It definitely hadn't looked like that the night before.

Mum was right. The den was definitely even messier than usual.

He peered out of the doorway to the landing, just in case – but he told himself that there was no way that Phyllis could have got out with the door closed.

Jacob turned back to face his den. His heart was pounding out of control. He scanned the devastation in his room, his forehead creasing in confusion. Then, his eyes fell upon the large beanbag in the corner of the room. It seemed to be raised slightly higher than usual, moulded in an odd, humped shape.

He stared.

It was rising and falling ever so slightly in a slow, steady rhythm. Stepping across the room to it and peering over the top, Jacob saw the reason.

Phyllis was curled up like a sleeping dog. She had wedged herself comfortably under the beanbag against the wall, and was still soundly snoozing away.

"I guess this felt a little bit like being squashed back in your rock," Jacob whispered in relief. He gave the back of her feathery neck a gentle stroke and peeled back the beanbag from on top of her.

Phyllis pulled her head out from the cosy space. She

72

opened her big, round eyes and squawked her familiar squawk.

"Thanks for not eating Steg and Rex," Jacob said to her.

Phyllis looked at him quizzically. She blinked a couple of times. Then, she let out a loud screech which made Jacob stumble backwards in surprise.

"What was that?" shouted Mum from downstairs.

Jacob mustered the quickest excuse he could think of. "Oh, just something in my game. Sorry, I had the speakers turned up too loud!"

Covering his lie, he quickly switched on his console and went straight to *Raider's Peril* to see if anyone was online. Gabi was there so he pulled on his headset, flicked away some loose bits of foam and joined her.

"Gabi, can you hear me OK?" he whispered urgently.

"Yeah, I can but you're quiet. I was waiting for you to come online. I was so excited last night, I could barely sleep! I told my stepmum we had plans to meet again today because she wanted me to help out around the

B&B. I don't think she suspected anything. Anyway, how are you? Is Phyllis OK?" she replied at speed.

"She's fine but she's nearly just given herself away with a noise so loud I'm surprised you didn't hear it down the street. And my den is looking more trashed than ever!"

"We need to meet!" said Gabi.

Chapter Eight

Gabi, Nakeisha and Faizal arrived together at Jacob's house.

"Jacob, your friends are here," Mum called up the stairs after answering the door.

"Can you send them up?" Jacob answered.

"Well, it wouldn't have hurt to come down and greet them," Mum said briskly. "Go on up, kids. You know where the den is. You'll have to excuse his mess. You know what he's like!"

They filed upstairs and knocked on the door to the den before entering. Inside, it was obvious what Jacob and his mum had meant. Model dinosaurs and bits of science experiment kits were littered around the floor. The globe was lying on its side on the desk. A couple of torn posters were hanging limply from the wall.

Jacob had his back to them. His arms were spread out

wide, holding his duvet like it was a big barrier. He shuffled and danced from side to side. He didn't turn around or explain, but he was sure that they could guess what was being contained behind the duvet. The squawking and flapping gave Phyllis away easily.

"What's going on?" asked Faizal.

"She keeps trying to jump or fly or whatever. I dunno if she's excited or annoyed or just wants to get out of this room. We can't keep her here much longer, though. She's going crazy!"

"Right," said Nakeisha. "Faizal's brought the dog coat and extendable lead again. Let's get Phyllis out and back down to the beach. We can decide what to do when we're somewhere out of the way."

"But we'll be seen," said Gabi. "It's too risky."

"I don't think we have much choice," Faizal observed. Phyllis flapped again behind the duvet. Jacob tried to use it to keep her in the corner. One wing caught a jar full of Jacob's favourite shells, sending them all crashing to the floor. Two landed in the bowl of water but most of the water had already been splashed out. It had formed a soggy patch on the carpet – at least that was what Jacob *hoped* the wet patch was...

"Come on," Nakeisha continued. "We'll keep to the bottom edge of the cliffs and head past the spot where we found her. There are the little crags and caves along there where we'll not be seen. Plus, it's drizzly and cold again outside. There'll be hardly anyone down on the beach today."

*

Not long later, the four had made it out of the house without Jacob's mum spotting Phyllis. As a precaution, they had bundled her up in the duvet and then abandoned it at the bottom of the stairs as they left. Jacob supposed that he'd get told off for that later.

He had grabbed his rucksack again, still partially packed from the day before. They had made it through the village, the gardens and down the steps to the beach without passing close enough to anyone to be noticed and, thankfully, there was no sign of Sam.

On the beach, they came to the rock which still had the impression of Phyllis' skeleton. To everyone's horror, it was now encircled with brightly coloured tape.

DANGER   DANGER   Property of Jurassic Coastal Museum   Pr
seum   Property of Jurassic Coastal Museum   DANGER

"Old Mister Penniket must have claimed it as his own already!" Faizal said.

Gabi led the way with Phyllis on the lead and the group picked up their pace. Every now and then, Jacob put his binoculars to his eyes and cast a glance around, like he was the official lookout.

All the way, Phyllis tried to pull towards the lapping waves of the sea. She flapped and wriggled. Luckily, her wings were pinned down by the dog coat and harness. At one point, she managed to poke the wings free from the coat for a proper attempt. She just about took off for a few metres before crashing back to the sand. She hadn't conquered the skill of flying just yet, but it looked like she was learning fast.

If anyone had seen them from a distance and been fooled into thinking that the gang were out walking a dog, they would have been mightily surprised to see the 'dog' leave the ground for a short distance and suddenly appear to grow a pair of wings from under its coat.

It was a miserable Sunday morning and, until that point, they had hardly seen another soul. Jacob took another cautionary look through the binoculars. No one was ahead of them, where the beach curved out of sight around the cliff. No one was out at sea – not even the occasional boat appeared on the horizon. Then, he looked back behind them.

"Uh-oh," he muttered.

"What?" Faizal asked.

"It's Sam," said Jacob, "and he's walking this way with old Mister Penniket. Run!"

They all broke into a sprint.

"I knew it – the traitor!" Faizal grumbled as they ran.

Gabi and Phyllis still led the way. Faizal, wearing his own trainers unlike the day before, was close behind, dodging the waves lapping along the shore. Nakeisha splashed through the edge of the water each time it crept into their path. Jacob followed clumsily with his rucksack bouncing up and down on his back.

Ahead, a large section of cliff rock jutted out onto the

beach and sprawled into the water like a jetty. They clambered up onto it and continued around the face of the rock formation. Each step took them further out of sight of Sam and Mister Penniket, and they were now raised up above the sand. By the time they reached a shallow opening in the side of the rock, only just big enough to be considered a cave, they were hidden well enough.

Clouds had started to swirl in the sky and a fine rain was falling. The overhanging rock and protruding sides of the cave meant that they were unlikely to be seen, but there wasn't a lot of room. At the end of the rock formation, the waves lapped at the stones. Gabi pinned the handle of the lead under a large rock and wheezed as she tried to catch her breath.

"Do you think he spotted us?" asked Nakeisha.

They all sat to gather their thoughts. Each of them perched on some wet rocks while Faizal stood and inspected his sand-splashed footwear.

"I think we were out of sight before they had a chance to notice us," said Jacob. "We were far enough away. I only saw them because I had the binoculars. We should be OK now."

"I can't believe he was with that evil old man," said Nakeisha.

"I can," sneered Faizal. "I told you – they're both as weird as each other."

"I wonder where they were going," Jacob thought out loud.

"Probably back to Phyllis' rock. But what exactly do *we* do now?" Gabi said between breaths. All four pairs of eyes turned to Phyllis as they struggled to come up with a plan.

"She keeps trying to pull towards the sea, you know," Nakeisha observed. Phyllis craned her neck out in the direction of the water, as if to reinforce the point. Not for the first time, Jacob thought she looked like her beak was in the air to catch a scent.

"Maybe she wants to swim," suggested Faizal.

"Maybe she wants to fly away somewhere," added Nakeisha.

"I don't want her to go," Gabi chipped in gloomily. Then, there was a silence.

Jacob considered their options. There was no way they could keep Phyllis – not after the events of the night before. There was no way they could keep her a secret, either. *What does Phyllis want to do?* he thought. He looked at her, wishing that she could somehow share her thoughts.

Phyllis was staring out at the sea. She raised her beak again, definitely appearing to catch a scent from the open water. Her usual squawking was reduced to more of a whining noise.

"I think she wants to be free," said Jacob quietly. The others looked at him and looked at Phyllis. They knew it, too. Gabi nodded slowly, a look of acceptance on her face.

"If we could let her go somewhere away from here, at least she'd be far from the fossil hunters, the museum, the tourists..." Jacob went on.

"Away from here would be great," agreed Nakeisha, standing up and peering round the headland to the beach, "but I think we have a bigger problem." She nodded in the direction of the rocks they had come over.

The others rushed to her side to look. Jacob felt a cold shiver run from his head to his toes.

The end of the rock jetty was now covered by lapping waves and, beyond it, the sea water was becoming deep and choppy. To either side of their cave, the cliffs adjoining them were too high to climb and the strip of beach that they had used to climb up from had vanished under churning waves. Everything on their rock was getting wetter, more slippery and more dangerous.

Gabi paced as far as she could across the small patch of rock that they were left with. "This is not good *at all.*" She spun round to look at the others.

"The tide's coming in. What are we going to do?" asked Jacob. "We're trapped!"

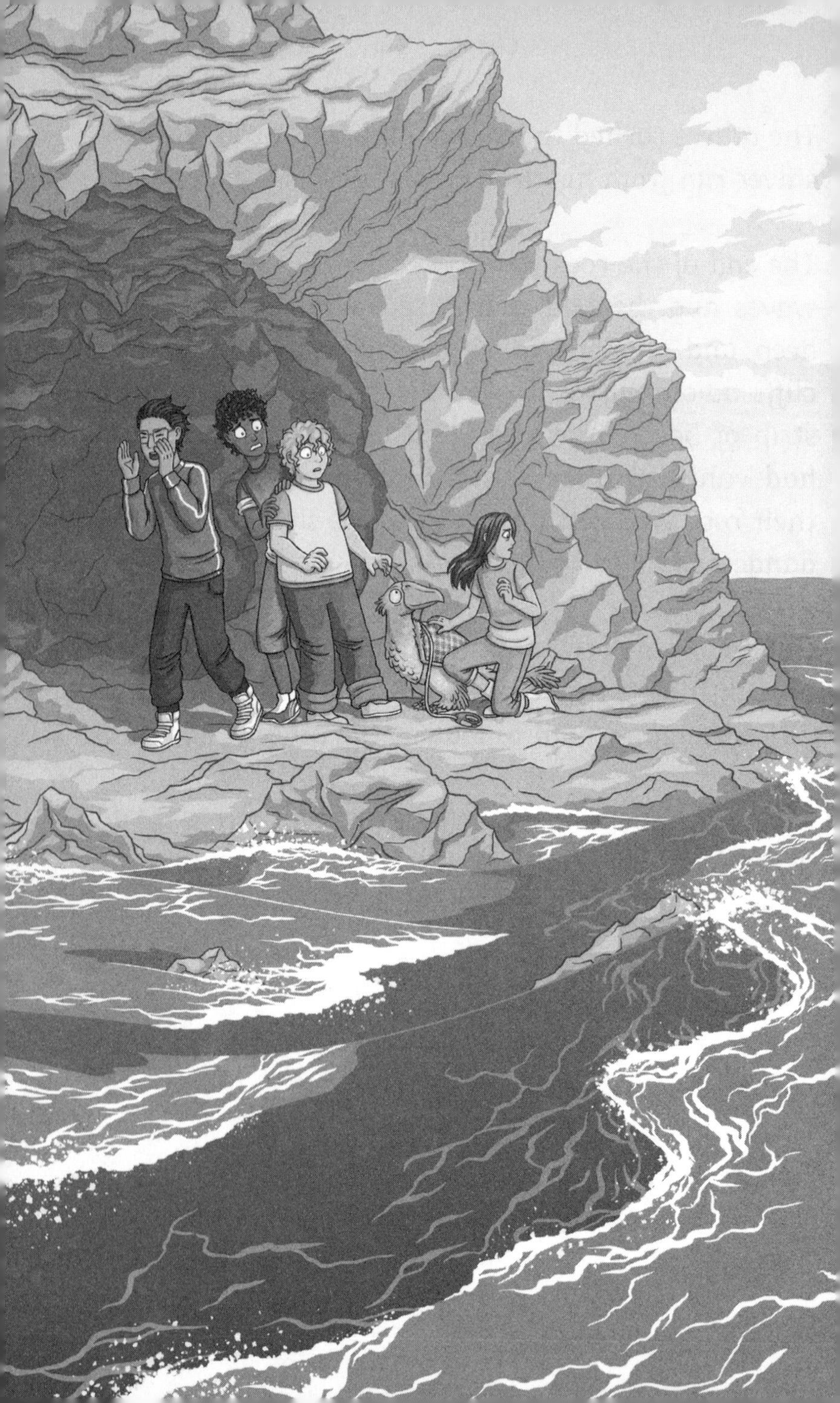

Chapter Nine

Jacob felt panic rising inside him. He tried to squash it down and quietly practised spelling dinosaur names to stay calm.

At low tide, the jagged cliff rocks either side of them were passable. Now, the water had crawled onto the beach and risen up them. There was no way out with the tide already in this far. At high tide, the large formation on which they stood might disappear under water completely.

Faizal was pacing around in the small area of rock in front of the cave. He was clearly starting to become anxious. "Help!" he shouted out, then again in the opposite direction. "Help! Anyone! Can anyone help us?"

Jacob recited the letters even louder in his head to drown him out but nothing was really working. He was not feeling at all calm.

Nakeisha looked up at the towering cliff face. The steep overhanging rocks made any upwards route impossible. She jumped as high as she could reach, grabbing at the rock, but it was pointless. There was nothing she could grip and no way up.

Phyllis watched them all with keen interest.

Gabi was clambering around the side of the headland which shielded them from view of the main beach. She was almost waist deep and couldn't see where she was putting her feet. Halfway through spelling 'Tyrannosaurus', Jacob saw her being pushed by the waves.

He stopped mid-word and shouted her back.

He was too late. Gabi's feet slipped out from under her and she seemed to fall in slow motion, toppling like a tower of building bricks.

As though his brain had gone into autopilot, everything happened before he had time to think about controlling his actions. Jacob dashed across the rocks and into the water until he, too, was almost up to his waist. He grabbed Gabi, who was clutching the side of the cliff and struggling to get back to her feet. He guided her up the craggy rocks to the platform, where Nakeisha grabbed her hand and helped to sit her down.

"What happened?" Jacob asked Gabi.

"I just lost my footing," Gabi muttered in reply. She put her hand to her head. "Everything went a bit blurry."

"You've done too much, Gabs," said Nakeisha. "You know what your stepmum says about overdoing it. She's right, you need to be more careful. We'll find a way out of this."

Suddenly, Jacob felt his brain switch back out of autopilot and the panic returned. The sea was closing in on them. The exertion of having to help Gabi had already sent his head spinning. Faizal was still shouting, Phyllis was squawking, the ocean was crashing against the rocks and all the noise seemed to echo around Jacob's brain.

He sat down in the sheltered cave opening and covered his ears, trying to block out the noise. Even when Nakeisha left Gabi's side to quieten Faizal, Jacob's head throbbed with fear. He lowered his chin to his chest and kept his hands over his ears. Everything was going on around him in a blur and it was hard to take it all in. He felt like curling up into a ball and hoping that it was all over and that he was back safe in his den. He didn't care any more if his mum was angry at him for the mess or for leaving the duvet in the hall. He just wanted to pull that soft, warm bed cover over his head and make everything quiet.

Phyllis was anchored to the rocks by the lead. She hopped from place to place as far as the reins would allow. She watched seagulls fly overhead. She wiggled and waddled and stamped her two clawed feet.

Meanwhile, Nakeisha grabbed Faizal by both arms. "Listen," she said to him. "I have an idea but I need your help!"

Faizal looked around at them all. Gabi was propped up against the rocks, exhausted. Jacob sat huddled just inside the cave with his knees pulled up to his chest. Faizal looked at Nakeisha.

"What if one of us wades out into the sea, with Phyllis attached to the lead?" she continued. "She's already trying to fly. If we can get her that bit further out and she starts flying up into the air, there's a chance that she'll be seen from the main beach. It could attract someone's attention to help us."

"No way, Keisha," Gabi coughed. She tried to sit up. "That's like using her as bait. If someone sees her, they'll take her away, not set her free."

"I think Keisha's right, Gabi," said Faizal. "It could be our only chance. If this tide comes in much further, we'll all be in the sea."

"There's no way Gabi should risk it again, though," said Nakeisha, "and I don't think Jacob is going to be able to either."

Under all the noise, Jacob heard her but didn't say anything.

"Then, it's you or me," Faizal said to Nakeisha.

"But I can't swim," said Nakeisha.

Faizal gaped at her in surprise. She had never told them this before.

"I'm so scared I'll drown. I just don't think I can go out there," she continued.

Faizal looked out at the approaching waves. He glanced down at his not-so-pristine-looking trainers.

Finally, he cast his eyes from Gabi to Jacob and back to Nakeisha.

"OK," he said. "Let's untie the lead from the rock. I'll give it a try."

Blinking away the fuzziness and understanding what Faizal was agreeing to do, Jacob began to unfurl himself. He tried to keep his breathing steady, picturing his fossils on the shelf of the den and counting them. He watched as Nakeisha handed Faizal the lead and removed Alfie's coat from Phyllis. Phyllis flapped her wings and seemed excited to be allowed the chance to move.

Gabi propped herself up on her elbows and watched through bleary eyes. Faizal and Nakeisha scrambled gradually around the rocks towards the beach, with Phyllis on the end of the lead. At first, she hopped across the wet cliffside behind them. Then, she flapped into the water and bobbed around as they made their way further around the edge. Without warning, she surged into the air and Faizal struggled to stay attached to the land as the waves crashed against him, threatening to knock him off balance. He clicked a button to allow the lead to extend as Phyllis pulled further away from him.

She flapped up into the air again and landed back on the surface of the water, repeating her effort again and again. Her squawking could be heard over the crashing waves. Finally, she stayed airborne for a few more seconds. It was her best bit of flying so far!

The waves jostled Faizal around on the rocks. He clung to the handle of the lead with both hands as it rose up into the sky with their living fossil on the end of it, and Nakeisha held the back of Faizal's jacket with one hand as she clung to the cliffside. As he wrestled with the lead, extended to its full length, he shouted again and dared to quickly wave one arm.

"Help! Help us!" His shouts were caught in the waves. Phyllis plummeted back to the surface and looked as exhausted as Gabi.

"Faiz!" Nakeisha screamed as a wave washed over Faizal, covering his head. Quickly, he popped back up through the surface of the water and desperately began to scramble back onto the land. His usually neatly combed hair was now flattened across his brow.

Eventually, with Nakeisha's help, he made it and collapsed onto the shrinking patch of uncovered rock that they had left. Phyllis squawked and flapped in protest as he pulled her to shore; Gabi grabbed hold of her and stroked her head gently, hushing her and giving her a comforting cuddle.

Jacob looked around. Between the four of them (or five, including Phyllis), they looked like they'd been shipwrecked or survived some kind of brutal storm – only they hadn't survived yet. They were still stranded. The water level was now even higher on the rocks at either side and the sea was making its way towards them along the rough jetty.

Maybe they were not going to get out of this at all. Jacob felt hot tears creeping into his eyes.

Suddenly, there was a shout from above.

"Who's down there? Faizal? Jacob? Is that you guys? Are you OK?"

The voice was Sam's. It was coming from somewhere above them, out of sight.

"We're stranded here. We need help!" shouted Nakeisha in reply.

"No, don't answer him," warned Faizal, gasping. "It's

Sam and he was with Mister Penniket, remember?"

"Don't be an idiot!" Gabi snapped. "It doesn't matter who it is. We need rescuing *now*. We need the help of whoever is there to help – Sam, Mister Penniket or whoever! They must be on the headland at the top of the cliff."

"Who's there with you?" Sam shouted down. They couldn't see him and perhaps he couldn't see them. "What was that thing you had hold of, Faizal? We saw you in the water. Was it a bird?"

They looked at each other, not knowing how to answer.

"It's a long story, Sam," Jacob shouted back. He felt like his autopilot brain was taking over again but this time, he made the choice to let it continue. "There are four of us down here. Keisha and Gabi are here, too. We really need some help. The thing you saw is... well, it's like a fossil... but it's come back to life. She's called Phyllis. We need to release her, but we're stuck. Can you help?"

Faizal, Nakeisha and Gabi looked at Jacob. He hoped that they weren't angry. He couldn't always be sure of people's expressions. He hoped that he had done the right thing.

There was no immediate reply.

"Sam?" Jacob shouted again. He wondered whether or not he had been heard. Was Sam still there?

"Yeah, we can help!" came a reply. "We can come down the steps further around the coast. They lead straight to the water but my uncle has a boat there. We'll be as quick as we can!"

Jacob looked at the others again. He wondered if they were thinking the same things as him. *A boat? His uncle?* Well, at least help was on its way – but what did it mean for Phyllis?

Chapter Ten

"Perhaps we should just let her go now, before they reach us," suggested Faizal.

Gabi was quickest to respond. "No! We can't! She can't fly properly. Even if she survived the tide coming in, then what? She'd be found by someone else. We need to get her somewhere further away – somewhere safe."

Phyllis cocked her head and looked at them. She stretched and lifted up her wings in what looked like a shrug.

"We might not have any choice, Gabs," said Nakeisha. As she spoke, she nodded out towards the sea. The others followed her gaze. They watched the swell of the water and, before long, a boat loomed into view. Almost immediately, it was within shouting distance of them, having come from just along the coast.

At the front of the boat, Jacob could clearly see Sam. Next to the boy was a man with a bushy beard wearing a scruffy, green cap. There was no doubt that it was Mister Penniket.

Faizal stepped in front of Phyllis protectively, as the boat slowed a little way out from the shore.

"We can't come any closer because of the rocks," Sam shouted to them. "Can you wade into the water and we'll throw some life jackets and a rope for you to hold on to?"

Jacob glanced at Faizal, who was standing with his feet planted firmly on the ground and his arms crossed like a bodyguard. Nakeisha, who had just admitted her fear of the sea, seemed to wobble with a new wave of panic. Jacob looked across at Gabi, fearing the worst. Instead, he saw a fresh look of determination in her eyes.

"I'm ready," Gabi announced. "Keisha, you need to be brave. And Faiz, you need to be more trusting and less stubborn. Jacob, you're the one we look up to. You always know the right thing to do. We're following your lead. Whatever else is going to happen, we need to get on that boat, we need to take Phyllis and we need to stick together."

They look up to me? Jacob heard those words above all others repeating in his head. He wasn't prepared to let his friends down.

Gabi's rallying call had the desired effect. Jacob stood up taller, pulled on his rucksack, grabbed Phyllis' lead and stepped along the rocks into the water. He tied the end of the lead around his waist, then reached his arm out behind him and beckoned for Nakeisha to join him. Everyone's feet were already paddling; the sea had covered their patch of rock. The boulders to either side were just peaks, everything else under water.

"Grab hold of each other," he instructed. "I'll lead. Keisha, hold my arm. I won't let go of you."

Gabi shot him a smile. "Faizal, go next. Hold on to Nakeisha and I'm holding on behind you. We can do this!"

Under Jacob and Gabi's instructions, they filed into line and began to wade further into the sea, feeling their way cautiously with every step below the water. Phyllis flapped wildly on her lead at the front. She bobbed on the surface, took off for a second or two every now and then, and splashed down again.

Mister Penniket had not said a word yet – or taken his eyes off Phyllis. As the group got closer, he heaved a thick coil of rope into the air. It unfurled and landed on the surface, a few metres ahead of them. When Jacob was close enough, he grasped the rope with his free hand and instructed Nakeisha to kick while they pulled themselves along the rope to the side of the boat.

Jacob helped the others up and over the edge, one at a time. Miraculously, Phyllis got the idea and propelled herself out of the water and onto the boat, too. Sam and Faizal leaned over and helped to yank Jacob up last of all. Mister Penniket told them to lift the seats and put on the bright orange life jackets that were stored there. He passed them a blanket each, which they wrapped around themselves as they sat down. No one had yet said anything about the flapping creature that was attached to the lead.

Sam broke the silence. "Are you all OK? What is that creature, then?"

They each chipped in with details as they recounted the tale – from finding Phyllis as a fossil to seeing her come back to life before their eyes and everything that had happened leading up to this point.

Through it all, Mister Penniket stood and listened as the boat bobbed from side to side. Occasionally, he shook his head. Numerous times, his tiny eyes widened and seemed to pop out from underneath his bushy eyebrows. At one point, he took off his cap and scratched his head. Phyllis hopped from the seat to the floor to the side of the boat, looking at everyone in turn.

"So, you see, Sam," Jacob finished off, "we just don't want to see Phyllis end up in the museum or get poked and prodded by scientists or archaeologists. She's real and she's alive and we just want to set her free somewhere safe."

Faizal chipped in. "Yeah, but obviously you've brought *him* from the museum for some reason," he said angrily, motioning towards Mister Penniket, "so I guess that's not going to happen now, is it?"

Sam looked at the man. "What do you think we should do, Uncle Alan?"

It took a moment to register with Jacob, then seemed to dawn one by one on the faces of them all.

"'Uncle Alan'?" Nakeisha said. "You mean, Mister

Penniket is your uncle?"

"Yeah," said Sam. "I've lived with Uncle Alan since I was little. I never really knew my mum or dad."

"So, that's why you're always around the museum and the fossil tours," Faizal said, as though his brain were struggling to keep up properly with what he was hearing.

Phyllis seemed to sense that a decision was about to be made and let out a squawk. She wore her cutest expression and looked – as they all did – to Mister Penniket. Gabi gave her a reassuring stroke.

"Well, well, well." His deep voice rumbled as he rubbed his beard.

Gabi bowed her head and looked prepared for the worst.

"You kids have found yourselves something pretty special, by the looks of it. She's quite a beauty. I've never seen anything like it before. Sam showed me the rock with the fossilised impression but I certainly wasn't expecting this."

"Please, sir," Nakeisha pleaded, "don't put her in the museum."

"Save your breath," Faizal said to her.

"The museum?" asked Mister Penniket. "A museum is not a place for living creatures. I think you kids are absolutely right. I think she needs to be free."

"What? Really?" Gabi's eyes lit up.

"Of course," he replied. "I don't know how this thing here has come to be, but that's not my business. I deal with fossils. I say let living creatures stay living in the present – even if this thing has come on a first-class ticket straight from the past."

The friends leapt out of their dripping wet seats, cheering and hugging each other. Phyllis joined in with the excitement with some hopping and squawking of her own.

The activity made the boat rock wildly. Jacob quickly dropped to his seat and clung on to it so as not to fall overboard.

"As for that exquisite bit of rock along the beach, there,

with the skeletal impression... I've never seen anything like that in all my years of fossil-hunting. Now, that will be a major catch for the museum. It'll bring more people to our door – goodness knows we could use the attention. Maybe then, poor old Sam here won't have to stick around helping me so often."

There was a brief moment of quiet while everyone thought about the man's words. Jacob thought that he saw Faizal and Gabi glance at one another.

"In that case," he asked, "what *shall* we do with her?"

Mister Penniket rubbed his chin. "It seems to me that this little lady keeps looking out towards the sea. Maybe that's the direction she fancies."

"She does keep doing that," Jacob added. "It's like she's catching a scent or sniffing for something."

"Maybe she can sense freedom," Gabi smiled.

Sam's uncle tugged on the peak of his cap and then took to the wheel of the boat. "No time to waste, then, if we're going on a mercy mission and then getting you kids all back onto dry land. Keep those blankets wrapped around you and hold on tight."

"But where can we set her free?" Sam asked his uncle.

Mister Penniket smiled. "I know just the place."

Chapter Eleven

The rocky coastline became smaller and smaller behind them in the distance as the boat powered through the waves. Phyllis seemed to become more and more animated as they travelled. Eventually, Jacob held onto her while Faizal and Sam worked together to fasten the lead to one of the seats.

When Jacob let go of Phyllis, she used the full extension of the remaining lead to flap her way up to the front of the boat. She hopped around and flew in short bursts. Each time, she landed back down on the front of the boat, prevented from going further by the dog lead but apparently approving of the direction.

"Where are we going?" asked Faizal.

"There are some islands out there," replied Mister Penniket over the hum of the boat's engine. "A couple of them have no inhabitants. Just greenery and nature."

It was not long before an island came into view. It

was like a small mountain rising from the sea to a green peak in the middle. There was no beach or much of a shore. It just seemed to be edged with rocks and covered in plantlife.

The boat began to slow as they got closer. Phyllis was so excitable, it was like she was trying to pull the boat closer to the island.

"I think she's found her destination," said Sam's uncle.

"I guess we have to say goodbye, then," Jacob said sadly.

Gabi gently put her arms around Phyllis, whispering to her. Faizal and Nakeisha followed, giving the creature a ruffle of her feathers and a stroke at the back of her neck.

Jacob was last. "I'm gonna miss you, Phyllis – even if you did trash my den! I hope you'll be safe and happy, though. We've been really lucky to meet you and we'll definitely never forget you."

They stepped back together and put their arms – and blankets – around each other.

"Ready?" asked Sam's uncle, as he held onto Phyllis and gave her a final inspection.

Through a snivel and a tear, they all nodded their agreement. The man took off Phyllis' harness and placed her on the side of the boat. She shook all her feathers and stretched her wings. Just as she was about to leap, she looked behind. Looking at the group, she gave one last blink of her big, bulging eyes and launched herself into the air.

Up she went, then sideways a bit, then – splash – down onto the water. Straight away, she was up and airborne again, like a pebble that had been skimmed along the surface.

Jacob took out the damp pair of binoculars from his sodden rucksack. He watched Phyllis reach the rocky edge of the island and passed the binoculars to Gabi.

"She's made it," Gabi announced. The group cheered again, but with mixed emotions now. A cloud of sadness hung over them at the thought of not seeing their new friend again.

Faizal took the next turn with binoculars. "Flippin' heck!" he yelled. "Am I seeing things or what?" He passed them to Nakeisha as the others squinted into the distance and wondered what he thought he'd seen.

"O.M.G.," Nakeisha gasped. "There's two of them! Phyllis has a mate!"

Everyone took a turn looking through the binoculars, including Sam and his uncle.

"I don't believe it," said the man as he passed them back to Jacob.

"Maybe that's why she was so excited about this direction!" said Gabi, breathlessly.

"Maybe that's what she was sniffing out all this time," suggested Jacob.

"Maybe they'll live happily ever after!" Nakeisha gushed.

"Just when we thought these couple of days could not get any crazier," said Faizal with a chuckle. Through the lenses of the binoculars, Jacob watched Phyllis rub her neck against the mate that she had found. It had the same feathery neck and the same bulgy eyes. Both of them padded their clawed feet up and down and wiggled their bodies from side to side.

Sam's uncle took off his cap again and scratched once more at the top of his head.

"In all my days..." he began, but tailed off, shaking his head instead. "I think we'd better get you lot back home before you catch your death." He pulled the peak of his cap back down over his forehead and turned back to the wheel of the boat.

*

Before the friendly sight of the mainland came back into view, the adventurers sat in the back of the boat, huddled together to keep warm.

"Thanks for your help, Sam," said Jacob.

109

"Yeah, thanks… and sorry for being hard work earlier," added Faizal.

"S'alright," said Sam.

"I gotta ask, though," Faizal went on, lowering his voice a little. "Does your uncle actually kill animals and keep them in your flat? Does he wear the skins after he's killed them?"

Sam laughed. "No, of course not. That's just a stupid rumour. He does create the museum exhibits. They might look like dead animals but they're just models – and I've never seen him hurt a living thing in all my life. The only animal skin is the one that's hanging on the wall in the museum."

"So, that's why you hang around the tours, then? 'Cause it's your uncle as the guide?" Faizal pressed.

"Well, yeah, and there's not much else to do when you don't have any friends. I always wondered what you guys were doing. You always look like you're having an adventure. I didn't mean to poke my nose in." It was as though he had read Faizal's thoughts.

"You ever played *Raider's Peril* online?" Faizal asked.

"Yeah, I love it!" Sam replied. "I just can't seem to find any fire opal weapons and it's hard raiding on your own."

Faizal looked at the others for any sign of objection. None came.

"We're all on there, too, and we've found the fire opal," he announced proudly to Sam. "Do you want to join our guild?"

"Definitely!" beamed Sam.

"Welcome aboard, then." Gabi patted him on the back. "You can join our adventures online as well as in real life. We *still* need a new guild name, though."

"What d'you think, Jacob? How about we call it 'Fossil Finders *Five*'?" suggested Faizal.

Jacob's eyes lit up. "Fossil Finders Five!" he repeated in agreement. "And when we've finished building our own stronghold, it can be 'The Fort of Phyllis'."

They all laughed as the familiar cliffs of the Jurassic Coast welcomed them back towards home.

Greetings

FROM THE

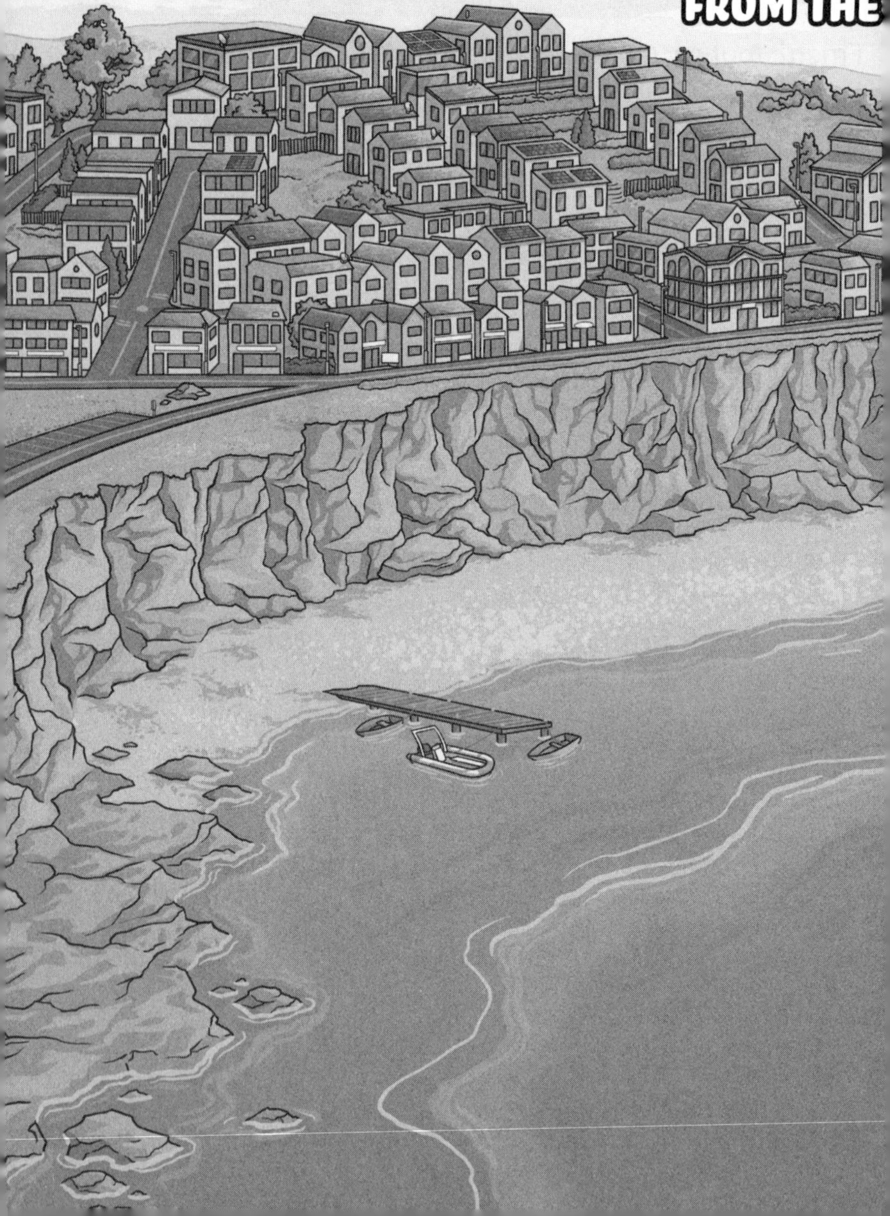

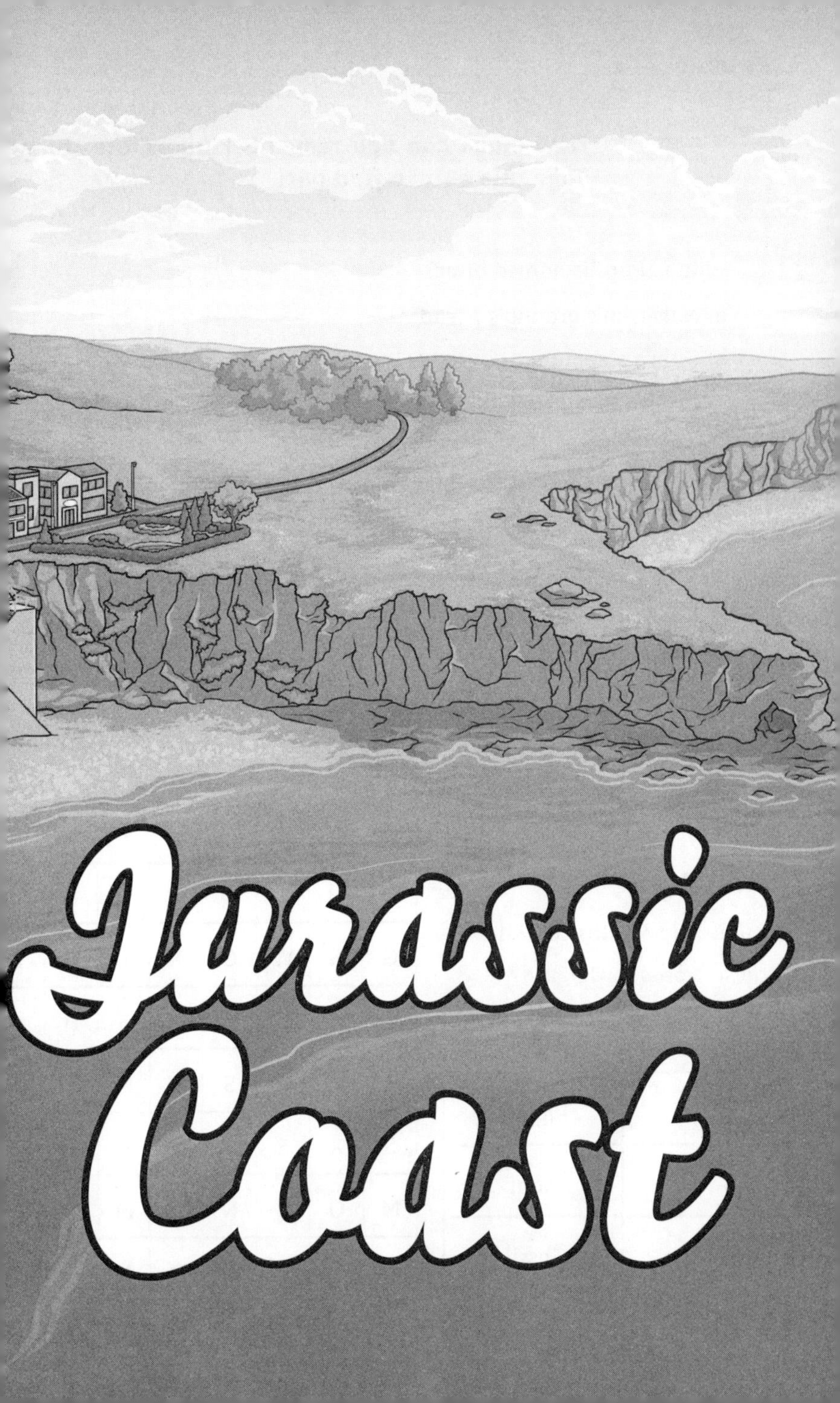
Jurassic
Coast

How much can you remember about the story? Take this quiz to find out!

1 Who is Phyllis named after?

a. Nakeisha's granny's friend

b. Gabi's stepmum

c. Jacob's favourite palaeontologist

2 What is the name of the online game that the children play?

3 Where do Jacob and his friends live?

a. Jurassic Park

b. Jurassic Period

c. Jurassic Coast

Answers 1. (a) 2. Raider's Peril 3. (c)

Challenge

Can you help Phyllis to find all these words in the grid?

Jacob	Phyllis
Gabi	Sam
Nakeisha	Fossil
Faizal	Finders

L	U	R	Q	T	F	P	U
G	S	W	O	X	L	P	L
N	A	K	E	I	S	H	A
Z	M	B	S	Y	M	Y	Z
S	X	S	I	P	P	L	I
M	O	U	N	B	M	L	A
F	S	R	E	D	N	I	F
J	A	C	O	B	R	S	L

Discussion Time

? Who is your favourite character from the story? Why?

? *Releasing Phyllis into the wild was the right decision.* Do you agree? Discuss your opinion.

? Do you think that the group make a good team? Can you find evidence from the story to support your ideas?

? What do you think the characters have learned?

Discover more from Twinkl Originals...

Continue the learning! Explore the library of Phyllis and the Fossil Finders activities, games and classroom resources at twinkl.com/originals.

Welcome to the world of Twinkl Originals!

Board books for ages 0-3

Picture books for ages 3-7

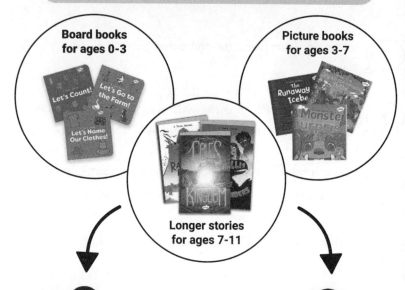

Longer stories for ages 7-11

twinkl Book Club

Books delivered to your door

Enjoy original works of fiction in beautiful printed form, delivered to you each half term and yours to keep!

1	Join the club at twinkl.com/book-club.
2	Sign up to our Ultimate membership.
3	Make your selection – we'll take care of the rest!

twinkl ORIGINALS

The Twinkl Originals app

Now, you can read Twinkl Originals stories on the move! Enjoy a broad library of Twinkl Originals eBooks, fully accessible offline.

Search 'Twinkl Originals' in the App Store or on Google Play.

 Download on the App Store

 GET IT ON Google Play

LOOK OUT FOR THE NEXT BOOK CLUB DELIVERY

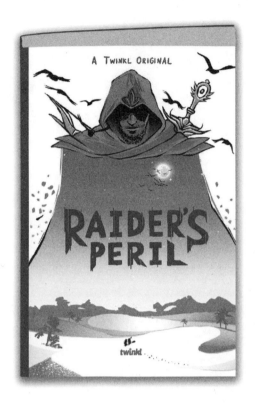

By day, Katka attends school with her friends but by night, she is Catanna Brittlestar, adventuring around the White Desert in search of precious gems. Then, the lines between her two worlds begin to blur – Katka thought Raider's Peril was just a game, but some players are raiding for real...

MARCH 2021

Can't wait? Get the digital version at twinkl.com/originals